PELL MELL

ADVENTURE ON THE RAILS

CAROL BIRD

Acknowledgements

Warm thanks to the gentlemen of the B&O Railroad Museum in Baltimore, keepers of America's railroading story. Well worth an afternoon's visit soon.

To Wayne Kirchhof, for your time, expertise, and the Pullman inspiration—you'll see glimpses of it here. A ride on your Walkersville Southern Railroad is a joy not to be missed.

And to the Nause-Waiwash Band of Indians, whose Annual Native American Festival in Vienna, Maryland let me sense, feel, and experience living traditions on this land.

Any mistakes found in the novel are mine alone. May the pleasures be yours to discover.

Chapter One
A Knock at Midnight

The knock came again—sharp and urgent—shattering the midnight silence of the house.

Penelope Mellors jerked upright, her heart hammering so hard it echoed in her ears. She took a deep breath. The smell of turpentine and old wood scented the air around her, wafting up from the workbench where she sat. Penelope, "Pell" as people called her, pressed a hand to her chest, willing it to slow.

"For goodness' sake, what fresh hell is this?"

Pell gently set down the O-gauge toy train car she held. It glinted under her work light, the gold filigree glowing. It wasn't finished—not yet. The interior upholstery still needed stitching, the tiny lamp sconces still needed wiring. But it was a little beauty—just like the toy Pullman sleeper cars she had made years ago to capture the imaginations of her son and nephew. *But who was this one for now that they were grown, John gone and no grandchildren…*

Another knock—this time harder. Pell tightened her smock around her waist, and rose with a grunt, knees crackling. She reached for the iron poker beside the fireplace, the habit of an older woman living alone, not paranoia. It had been years since anyone had come to her door uninvited. Especially at midnight. Especially someone who couldn't be bothered to call first.

Pell moved through the house in her slippers, her paint-flecked smock sweeping against the worn wooden floorboards, each step stirring faint dust motes in the glow of the moonlight slipping through the curtains.

The knock came again, and she winced.

"I'm coming, I'm coming," she muttered.

Pell flipped on the porch light, opened the inner door, and peered through the screen. A figure stood on the porch, face turned away from the light, a hand half-raised to knock again.

"Ned?" she said, blinking. "Is that you? What in the world?"

Her nephew Ned looked scruffy, drawn, and much too pale. His shirt was wrinkled, his jacket draped over a dark backpack. His eyes darted like a hunted animal.

"Yes, it's me, Aunt Pell. Please let me in."

She unlatched the screen and opened the door. Ned stepped in, locked the door behind him, flipped the porch light off, then stood and took a deep breath.

"Ned, what is going on?"

"I don't have time," he said, stepping past her into the front hallway. "I mean—I don't have long. Let's go into the kitchen, away from the windows, and I'll explain everything."

Ned flicked off the hall light as he went, Penelope trailing behind.

In the kitchen, the low hum of the refrigerator was the only sound besides Ned's ragged breathing. Ned sank into a chair and dropped the dark backpack next to him. He ran both hands through his hair. Pell stood with her hands on her hips, looking him over. He looked older than thirty-six, but younger than death. Something was badly wrong.

"When was the last time you ate something?"

"This morning. I sure could use a cup of coffee."

Pell began making coffee and pulled sandwich fixings from the refrigerator. The rich aroma filling the room was a small comfort against the growing tension.

"Okay, so what is this about? Is your father okay?"

Ned nodded. "Yes, yes, he's fine. I mean, you know he's not mentally the same, but he has his home health aide living in now. Asks for Mom once in a while as if she is still with us, which is gut-wrenching, but then he forgets he asked. Seems content to watch TV and take a long walk now and then. This isn't about Dad."

Penelope set a sandwich down in front of him and took a seat. The weight of the moment pressed down on her. Years of quiet evenings spent in this kitchen, and now this — a secret passing to her, heavy with danger.

"Well then, what? You're always welcome here, of course, but you scared the wits out of me coming at this hour."

Ned took a bite and hesitated, chewing. In the kitchen's warm light, with the coffee brewing, he looked almost human again.

"I know. It's late. I'm sorry. But Aunt Pell, you have to promise me that you won't tell anyone what I'm about to tell you. I need your help. You're the only one I can trust at this point."

"What is it, Ned? Do you need money? You know since John passed, I plan to give you everything anyway, so…"

"They know," he said finally. "The board members I've been investigating. They've been robbing the company. I was preparing to go to the Feds with it, but someone tipped them off. I'm not sure who—not all of them, just the ones who—look, Aunt Pell, I shouldn't even be here, but I didn't know who else to trust. I have a plan, but I really need your help."

She raised an eyebrow. "Try saying that again, but slower. And start with who 'they' are."

Ned took a breath. "The damn railroad board—the North and South Pulp and Paper Railroad board. Or most of them. The ones who've been bleeding the company dry. Kickbacks, ghost contracts, fake subsidiaries. I started putting it all together six months ago. I was going to blow it open, but someone inside anonymously warned me, or threatened me really. Wrote that, if I pushed it, I might not make it to the whistleblower meeting. Said there'd been… accidents before."

Pell's hands went still on her coffee mug. She studied him—not just the fear in his voice, but the steel underneath it. This wasn't a man losing his mind. This was a man who had seen something rotten and decided to burn it out. She was proud of him. *If only her husband George were here to help, if only John...*Pell pushed the thoughts down and focused on Ned.

"You're the CEO," she said. "Don't you have some kind of protection?"

"That's the joke," he said. "They think I'm the idiot son who got the job out of pity. They've been running things behind my back for years. And now that I've poked the nest, I have to disappear. Just for a while. Until I can figure out how to take them down properly. So, as far as possible, I want to make them think they got me, or at least that I just lost my nerve and cut out."

He reached into his bag and pulled out a thick envelope. "This is why I came. I can't hold onto my stake anymore. It's too visible. Forty percent. I'm transferring it to you. Clean and legal. I drew it all up myself. You don't have to do anything with it—just sit on it, and don't let anyone know you have it. That way you can stay safe."

Penelope stared at the envelope. *Should I tell him? Surely he has to understand, given my age…*

"Ned—"

"I trust you Aunt Pell," he said, eyes on hers, almost pleading. "I always have. You're the only one left."

Penelope opened the flap and thumbed through the pages. Legal, notarized, sealed. All the right phrases, as far as she knew. He'd been planning this for more than a day.

"And what do you expect me to do with this?" she asked softly.

He shrugged. "Keep it safe. Maybe if we work together, we can keep the company alive. I was trying to save it, Aunt Pell. It could still be worth saving. A lot of people depend on it."

She set the papers down gently and looked at him—this nephew who'd been her favorite, the closest thing she had left to a son. Her heart ached in places she thought had long gone numb.

"You were always going to inherit everything anyway," she said.

"I know. Thank you. But I really wish John was still here instead. He would help make sure it didn't all go to the wrong people."

Nodding, Pell signed without ceremony, the pen gliding along the line. Outside, the wind picked up, rattling the windowpanes like whispered threats from the dark beyond.

Ned tucked the empty envelope back into his bag and took out a smaller, letter-sized envelope.

"Aunt Pell, this is a letter introducing you to a man named David Hadley. He's been a good friend for years. He doesn't know everything about the board's scams, but he has some pretty good ideas about what's going on and can get in touch with me in an emergency. He's a little, uh, unconventional, but he knows the railroad like the back of his hand. You can find him squatting in the old executive car at the Maine railyard. You can trust him."

Ned stood and walked to the front door with his backpack, Penelope beside him.

"Ned, where will you go?" she asked.

He turned and gave her a hug. "It's safer if you don't know. I'll reach out when I can. Remember, don't tell anyone you saw me or have the stock. If you need to do anything with it, like vote in a stockholders' meeting, you can do it anonymously. I've explained everything in a note with the papers."

He put his hand on the doorknob, paused, then turned back again.

"If I don't make it back—"

Penelope's heart wrenched and she cut him off. "Please don't say that. Just don't get yourself killed. I'll be furious if you do."

Ned's smile was tired but real. "Then I guess I better not."

And then he was gone.

Pell quickly locked the door behind him, then returned to the kitchen to clean up. She took the papers to her workshop and put them into the wall safe her late husband George had installed many years ago. She remembered teasing him about it—as if they had anything of value to put in a safe back then. That had certainly changed. George might have been a little sexist, calling her crafting of miniature masterpieces, "that little hobby of yours," but he was brilliant and had taken loving care of them all.

"Well George, I bet you would have known just what to do for poor Ned."

Penelope spun the combination lock. "By the way, if I never told you, you were right about the safe."

Chapter Two
The Man in the Pullman

Pell awoke at six-thirty sharp, as she always did—whether or not there was anywhere to be. Today, there wasn't. But her mind was already crowded: plans to make, things to think through.

Pale morning light shone dimly through the lace curtains. She sat up, gathered her thick silver hair, and twisted it into the neat knot she favored to keep it out of her eyes. Her joints complained after the late night, but she ignored them the way some people ignore the slow drip of a leaky faucet.

She dressed with her usual efficiency: navy slacks, cream blouse, sturdy walking shoes. No one had ever accused her of fussing with fashion, but she knew how to look like she belonged—in a boardroom or a barn.

Over oatmeal and half a grapefruit, Pell unfolded the letter Ned had handed her the night before. The paper was creased from travel; the handwriting was sharp, hurried. She read it twice. The gist: *David Hadley. Knows the railroad. Knows me. Trust him.*

Pell set the letter down. She could stay home and keep Ned's papers locked away like some dutiful aunt in a television drama. It was tempting. After all, she was getting to be an old woman. What was left? Everyone who mattered gone. But in her mind's eye rose the woman she used to be—mother, wife, artist of delicate miniatures, community leader. She had lost too much of her heart in recent years, and let too much slide, if she was honest about it. And Ned needed her.

Before she could talk herself out of it, Pell decided: she would go to the railroad. She would meet David Hadley. By ten o'clock she had a flight to Maine booked for the next afternoon, and a hotel room as close to the railyard as she could find.

The day was for packing—and for finishing the toy Pullman executive car. In her workshop, morning sun warming her hands, she sewed the last scrap of velvet upholstery, brass fittings catching the light. By late afternoon, it was done. The little car gleamed: varnished wood veneer, tiny, shaded lamps in the salon, fold-down berths complete with miniature pillows. Tomorrow it would be packed in a padded box for the trip.

The next day, after a minor delay on the flight from North Carolina, Pell landed in Bangor. She rented a car for the long drive to Eastport, headquarters of the North-South Pulp and Paper Railroad. By evening, she had checked into a modest hotel and was eating a surprisingly cheap lobster dinner at the attached diner.

The next morning, armed with Ned's letter and her most confident stride, she walked to the railyard. The May air was chilly but bright, touched with the salt of the sea and the diesel of barges working the nearby docks.

Where she had expected a postcard relic of railroading, Pell found the street ending at a squat yellow building from the 1970s—flat, sealed windows, the "futuristic" energy-efficient style of its day. She'd never liked it, and time hadn't been kind. The washed-out sign by the glass door read: *North South Pulp and Paper Railyard Office.*

The building backed against a tall wire fence. Beyond it stretched the yard, parallel to the water. A blue-and-yellow diesel engine inched freight cars beneath a high conveyor reaching from a moored barge, spewing pulp into each open freight car.

Inside, the yardmaster—his nameplate confirming the role—sat behind a Formica counter, focus flicking between his screens and the single headphone over his left ear. He had the look of a man permanently behind schedule.

"My name is Penelope Mellors," she said, offering what she hoped was a disarming smile. "I have important papers for David Hadley. I was told I could find him here?"

The yardmaster looked blank for a beat, then something flickered. "Oh, you mean Dead Head. Might be around. You can look."

He jerked his head toward a young man in overalls filling a thermos. "Derek, walk her over to the Pullman."

Derek led her through the gate and into the yard, away from the loading operations. The entire place looked weary: the freight cars were marked with graffiti, weeds pushed up through gravel, trash drifted in the wind. Pell thought it looked as run-down as she felt.

"Mind your feet," Derek called back. "And don't walk between the rails. Dangerous if you trip. Always walk to the side."

Pell stepped clear, feeling faintly embarrassed.

Then she saw it.

The Pullman sat high on black-painted iron wheels nearly as tall as she was. Faded blue and maroon paint peeled in great curling sheets, a rust streak like an old scar ran down one side. The long, elegant line of windows, though clouded with grime, were at least unbroken.

Eighty-five feet long, ten feet wide, with rounded roof and ornate ironwork on the rear porch, the car still held the grace of the Gilded Age. Beneath the dirt, the lovely bones of an aging beauty waited. Pell felt the small thrum of satisfaction: her miniature had captured it exactly.

"Okay, this is it," Derek said. "DH should be around somewhere. You all set?"

"I'm fine, thank you. And I'll be sure not to walk between the rails on the way back."

He gave her a thumbs-up and left.

Pell climbed the three metal steps at the rear of the car, heaving her bag up first. The oval glass in the door was etched with a delicate pattern, dulled by dust. Unlocked. She slid it open, knocking and calling. No answer.

Overcome with curiosity, Pell stepped inside. Dust, and the fading of age, softened everything, but beauty still showed through: varnished mahogany paneling, gilt scrollwork, a Persian hall runner along the narrow passage, the curving salon windows lighting up the far end.

Her fingertips traced the trim as her mind filled with scenes: Hollywood starlets with piled hair and arched brows, Gilded Age millionaires in stovepipe hats, wives in furs draped with pearls. Avarice wrapped in elegance—but still, a part of her envied the slower pace, the assumption of comfort and a little romance. The old car might not be what she once was, but it would be a shame to waste what was left.

Pell was about to step further in when a man ducked through the doorway into the passageway in front of her. Pell startled, the close quarters suddenly smaller. This had to be Dead Head. He was tallish and lean, wearing a scuffed work jacket. Hair overdue for a trim. A graying beard that looked like it had lost a fight with a dull razor months ago.

"Who the hell are you?" he said.

"I might ask the same," Pell shot back. "I knocked. No one answered."

"So, you came in anyway?" His voice was flat. "This is my place."

"I thought it was the company's place. You look like a squatter."

He bristled. "Squatter? Lady, I've got more time in this car than—"

"Without soap or elbow grease, apparently."

That earned the faintest smile before he caught himself. "Ah. I'm guessing you're Ned Talmadge's Aunt Penelope. Name's Hadley. David Hadley."

He stepped forward, offered her a square, tanned hand. Pell took it. "That's right. I'm Penelope Mellors."

He nodded once. "That's better. People call me Dead Head."

"Do they now? Seems harsh, but if the shoe fits…"

"No, Ma'am. A dead header's company staff hitching a passenger run to get to where they're needed."

"Ah. Got it. I think I'll stick with DH, if you don't mind. You can call me Pell. Now that we're properly introduced, I have a letter from Ned."

She handed it over. DH read it, folded it neatly, slid it back into the envelope.

"That's his signature. Guess that makes you all right. You know where Ned is? He okay?"

Pell shook her head. "The short answer is, I'm not sure. But let's sit—we have a lot to go over." "Think you could scare up a cup of coffee for an old woman? I brought bear claws from the diner." She held up a white paper bag.

That got her another half-smile.

"I'll make us some coffee."

They sat at the cherry dining table, which currently doubled as a cluttered desk. Between sips and bites, DH explained that he and Ned had become friends several years ago, when Ned spotted the old executive car overgrown with weeds on the siding where it is now.

"He wanted to restore it and get it on the rails again. It was a labor of love, a hobby for us both. We got it to the state you see." Pell raised a brow.

DH continued, "Yeah, I know it looks rough, but the mechanicals are sound now and we added a generator so it can sit independent of connection to electricity from the engine. But when Ned moved into the CEO role, I guess he got busy and pretty much stayed down in North Carolina. Came up a few times to say hello, but we didn't get anything more done on the car."

Pell just nodded. Ned had always loved trains, big or little. So had John but not like Ned. She remembered the summer her brother in law had taken both boys with him to ride the train out of North Carolina here, to Maine. He heart pained remembering how John practically danced around her, waiting for his Uncle Victor and cousin Ned to pick him up for the ride to the railyard to start the trip. It was the highlight of their summer vacation.

This was long before her sister died, and Victor Talmadge began to slowly lose ground to Alzheimer's, finally passing his share in the railroad, and endorsement for a position to Ned, at that time a newly credentialed lawyer who had just passed the bar in North Carolina.

When DH was finished speaking, Pell asked, "What exactly does the railroad do? I know in broad terms of course but…"

DH walked around the table to the vintage map framed on the dining car's wall. He explained the work of the North South Pulp and Paper Railroad in terse, general terms pointing out landmarks on the old map as he went.

"This map is circa 1910, as you can read under the rosette, but for the most part, it's still accurate. We're here at the Maine railyard." He poked the spot.

"Pulp comes down to us on barges from mills up north. You probably saw the cars being loaded for the weekly run South."

His finger traced down the tracks. "The train travels across these two bridges, through the tunnel in Appalachia, and then through the Tobewanaki reservation here. The company pays road passage fees to the tribe to pass through. A lot of the rail workers are from the tribe and have been for generations.

Pell asked, "All this darker section indicates the reservation boundaries?"

DH nodded. "Once we get down to North Carolina, we make stops to deliver pulp to the paper plants here and here. One specializes in newsprint and the other in shipping containers. The train stay overnight at the railyard in North Carolina to fuel up and board fresh crew if needed. On the way back, we pick up the newspaper rolls and shipping container paper for the run back North, delivering that stuff to the press and plants that use it. Unless there's a problem, the whole route usually takes about ten days, if you count weekends."

Pell took a picture of the map to look at in detail later and asked, "What kind of problem?"

DH shrugged. "Trees or rocks across the track, maybe equipment failure. Long time ago, could have been a train robbery, but it's been over fifty years since we carried passengers to rob. Nobody wants a bunch of pulp."

"I'd like to see it for myself," Pell said. "A run from here to North Carolina and back. In this car, if we can get the restoration finished."

DH shrugged and gave a wry laugh. "I know some guys that can help get her up to snuff if you have the money to pay for it. The problem is, you'd have to get the company to say yes. They're not in the habit of letting people joyride. Especially people I know."

"Not in great standing?" Pell asked.

He shrugged. "Drank too much. Said too much." He looked at her cagily. "And the company doesn't much like anyone who uses the word union."

Pell gave DH a long look. A red flag flapped in her mind about the drinking. Too much of that was a deal-breaker, and DH clearly had reservations about her. Really, who wouldn't? He would be a fool not to be cautious.

She said, "And since you know I have Ned's stock in the railroad, you're worried I'll throw you out? Or be an anti-union spy?"

"Crossed my mind."

"I'm not going to," Pell said flatly. As I see it, if we're going to help Ned and find out what is going on with this company, we're going to have to trust each other. In fact—want a job? Contingent, of course, on you being done with drinking too much and my getting use of this car somehow."

DH raised an eyebrow. "A job doing what?"

"First, help me find out how to help Ned. Second, get this car fixed up and determine if this railroad's worth saving. Last, but not least, get the bad guys, if we can."

"Is that all?" DH shook his head, beard wagging back and forth. "Oh, what the hell, I'm in. Not doing much else anyway."

Pell rose and reached out to shake his hand. "Good. I'll be back tomorrow afternoon. Tonight, I need to figure out how to get the company to let me use this car. I have an appointment with the operations brass tomorrow morning."

"Better you than me. Good luck."

"One last thing. Ned might have told you this already but it's vital no one knows I have his company share, or that I'm his aunt. As far as you know, I'm just an excentric, old train enthusiast and you're working for me because it looked like easy money."

DH gave a nod. "Understood. I don't plan on telling anyone anything."

Pell dug around in her bag. "Do you have a vehicle?

"Yes, my old truck. But it's been sitting on empty for a while."

"Here is five-hundred. Consider it an advance. Get your truck going, get some food in here, and get some diesel in the generator."

DH folded the money into his pocket and gave her another of his slow nods. "See you tomorrow Boss."

That night in her hotel room, Pell sat with her laptop, digging through company press releases, board member bios, and old news clippings. According to all this, the North-South Rail was a rock-solid venture, profitable and growing. A good buy for the most risk-adverse investor. Not exactly what Ned said, or she saw at the railyard today.

Somewhere in the fine print was the angle she needed to negotiate for the Pullman car —something the company couldn't refuse without looking foolish. She stayed up past midnight, the buzz of purpose in her veins.

Chapter Three
The Box on the Table

Penelope Mellors believed in two things above all: strong coffee and well-laid plans. She'd had both this morning, in that order.

At 9:30 she packed the padded box she had carried from North Carolina, set it carefully on the passenger seat, and drove through a fog-softened morning toward the Maine headquarters of the North South Pulp and Paper Railroad. The railyard itself had disappointed her—too shabby, too ordinary—but the headquarters building lifted her spirits the instant it appeared out of the mist. Maybe there was hope for this old railroad.

The mansion was a confection in pale granite, complete with towers at either end and bowed windows gazing out over a restless gray Atlantic. A broad flight of stone steps rose to a deep wraparound porch furnished with black iron tables and chairs for outdoor dining. The double doors, framed in leaded crystal, gleamed beneath a brass plaque announcing the railroad's name in tasteful serif letters.

"Better," Pell murmured. "Much better."

She heaved open the heavy door and stepped inside. The entry hall was round and soaring, anchored by twin staircases that curved upward like mirrored ribbons. A crystal chandelier threw fractured light over polished marble. At the left sat a receptionist behind a curved wooden desk—computer monitor, printer, and phone looking slightly embarrassed to be there. A velvet claw-foot couch with carved arms offered seating.

The receptionist, a young woman in the universal navy blazer of her trade, looked up.

"May I help you?"

"Yes. I'm Penelope Mellors, Railroad Heritage Foundation. I have a ten o'clock with Alan Granger."

A polite pause, then: "One moment, please. You're welcome to sit."

Five minutes later Pell was ushered through tall double doors into a dining-room-turned-conference-hall, its décor lovingly preserved in the 1910 grandeur of the mansion's first owner. The long mahogany table smelled faintly of lemon polish.

Around it sat three men and two women, their fixed half-smiles betraying that they had been told to hear out a proposal. Pell noted, wryly, that business must be slow if five executives could spare a full hour for her.

Mr. Granger rose—his suit was very fine, his belly less so—and introduced her. Pell smiled as if she had brought pie to a church social and placed her box on the table.

"Thank you for seeing me. I'll get right to it. As you may know, I'm with the Railroad Heritage Foundation, a national network of enthusiasts who love the great era of rail travel. I count myself firmly among them.

"We also know that the North South Pulp and Paper Railroad turns one hundred and twenty-five in two years. Congratulations. In an age when so many private lines have folded, it's heartening to see such a survivor."

There was a murmur of acknowledgement. Granger smiled faintly but gave the barest sniff, the look of a man already wondering when this would be over.

Pell caught it—and decided it was time to use her secret weapon. She opened the padded box and lifted the gleaming HO scale model of a Gilded Age Pullman executive car. Its brass fittings caught the chandelier's light.

A ripple of surprise passed around the table.

"This," Pell said, "is a model of your original executive car, built in 1899 to court foreign investors for the southern extension. The real car still exists. It's in your yard right now."

One of the women, beautiful and dressed in a sharp cranberry suit, frowned.

"You mean that wreck? The one with raccoons in it?"

"Only one raccoon," Pell said sweetly, "and he's been evicted."

There were a few chuckles. Mr. Granger leaned forward, half-asking with his eyes if he might touch the car. Pell snapped on the model's interior lights and handed it to him.

"Open the roof," she said. "The berths fold down."

The little car worked its spell. Executives peered into the miniature windows, slid doors back and forth, chuckled like children. Pell let them.

"I propose to restore the real car to its original condition—mahogany paneling, brass fixtures, silk drapes—at my own expense. Once complete, I'd like to take it on a round trips from Maine to North Carolina, showcasing your heritage and your current operations. Invite reporters, local officials, photographers. All with you approval of course. It's positive press, goodwill, and, frankly, a powerful way to woo investors—just as it once was."

Cranberry Suit leaned over the model. "Think we could go for a ride? I'm Marissia Sadler, by the way. Head of Public Relations."

Pell nodded but before she could say anything, the balding man beside Marissa snapped, "Forget that! The real question is, why would you pay for all this yourself?"

"Because I'm a sentimental fool," Pell said. "Because I love trains. And because it's the right thing to do. But more to the point—it's free advertising, first for you and second, for the Heritage Foundation. The car remains property of the company. All I ask is permission to restore it, ride it, and bring along one experienced railroad man, as my employee, to keep us on schedule."

"Who?" Granger asked.

"David Hadley."

That drew an exchange of glances, a faint sigh from Cranberry Suit.

"I feel obliged to warn you," Granger said. "He's been… difficult. Still, if you want him, we certainly have no issue with you taking him off our hands."

"I expect he can be a bit difficult," Pell said evenly. "That's why I want him. I don't need a PR minder. I need someone who knows the line, the people, and—let's be blunt—how and where to dump the toilets."

That earned a couple of startled laughs. Pell let the silence stretch. The model rolled slowly down the table, each executive taking a turn with it.

At last Granger said, "It's an intriguing idea. Legal will have to draft a contract and consider risk management—no liability to the railroad, of course."

"Of course. But it's a win-win. No cost to you, full credit to you, and a reminder that this railroad still exists and is open for business. Say yes, and I'll have the restoration underway in a week."

Granger nodded. "How long are you in town?"

"Until I get things settled here. I'm at the Harbor House near the yard. I'll leave my number with your receptionist."

"Very well. We'll be in touch."

Pell packed the model away, thanked them for their time, and stepped back into the cool fog. She allowed herself a private smile. They thought they were humoring an eccentric old woman. Exactly as she intended.

Back at the hotel, Pell traded her skirt and jacket for jeans, a tailored flannel shirt, and light boots. She picked up burgers and pie from the diner and, after checking in with the office, carried them to the Pullman.

The door swung open to reveal a different David Hadley. Beard clipped, hair trimmed, clean shirt. Pell blinked in surprise: he was, in fact, rather handsome.

"Practical shoes," he said, eyeing her boots. "About time."

Pell shot back, "You found a barber. About time."

There was the half smile again.

"Better be nice," Pell said. "I brought burgers and pie." She moved to the dining room and set out the food while DH brewed coffee and offered her a cold bottle of water from the newly humming fridge.

"I got propane hooked up," he said, tapping the stovetop. "Kitchen's alive again. Even the freezer works."

Between bites, Pell told him about the meeting. "They'll get back to me after legal has a go at it. I have a feeling it'll be yes but wrapped in a pulp car's worth of paperwork."

DH almost laughed. "Good one."

"Thanks. I'm working on my railroading vocabulary."

When the food was gone, Pell set the padded box on the table and unwrapped the model railcar again. The tiny sconces glowed.

DH's eyes widened and he reached for the little Pullman. "You built this?"

"I sure did. It's my blueprint. That's how I want to restore this car."

He rolled it gently across the table, peering inside. "I know some guys who could get it done."

"Excellent," Pell said. "That way, if the rail execs give me the green light, we'll be ready. Now, since I passed the footwear inspection," she said, "how about a tour? Inside and out."

"A tour it is." DH began clearing the plates.

DH started with the sleeping rooms, yanking down the folding berths in each compartment. A puff of musty air escaped like the car had been holding its breath for a century. For a few beats, it was just the two of them and the Pullman—no railroad, no worries for Ned, no clock ticking somewhere else.

"These mattresses have fought—and lost—many battles," Pell said, wrinkling her nose.

"Yeah," DH replied. "We can haul them out today if you want."

"I more than want."

He tapped one with a finger, as if it might retaliate. "Same size Amtrak still uses. You could order new ones straight from the supplier. Sheets too. Vintage-approved."

Pell's mouth curved. "If we get the green light this week, I'll handle the order myself. Could even pick them up, if I can track a source. If not Amtrak, maybe a yacht outfitter."

"Two outfitters I know in town. Not cheap."

"Nothing is. But a proper bed is non-negotiable."

He moved on, pushing open a narrow door. "Each sleeper's got a bathroom—shower, folding sink, hot water. Runs on propane. Haven't tested it yet." He gave her a deadpan look. "But what's life without a little risk?"

They moved together through the compartments, their rhythm easy, playful. DH liked this version of Pell. For her part, Pell saw the boy still alive deep inside the dour man she had first met.

In the central salon, Pell leaned against a broad window. "This space is a real treasure. Convertible to sleep two more passengers or just sit here and admire the scenery. Tiny washroom to the side. You might need yoga training to fit comfortably."

DH nudged a folding table. "It's like a Swiss army knife, only made of steel and wood. Watch this." With a twist and a click, a panel revealed a hidden storage cubby. Pell gasped.

"I feel like we just unlocked a secret level," she said. "That is a perfect place for a safe, isn't it? Is there somewhere around here to get one?"

DH said, "Hardware store maybe. Adding it to the list."

She ran her fingers along the built-ins. "Everything's in working order. The mechanics purr, so thanks to you and Ned for that. It just needs a deep clean—industrial-grade, like a spa day for a hundred-year-old lady. And of course, painting."

"The usual guys I know mainly work on electrical and carpentry," DH said. "But someone around here will know someone who knows someone who can make her sparkle."

In the kitchen, DH flung open cupboards and rapped the stainless sink. "You could cook a Thanksgiving turkey in here, if you were brave. Or, realistically, a ham."

Pell laughed. "A tiny turkey, then?"

"Fine, maybe Cornish hens," DH admitted. "Back in the day, they made do. But apparently, they liked to eat like kings while doing it."

Next was the secretary's cubby. A metal, child-sized desk and chair bolted next to the window. A dusty black phone with a conic earpiece bolted to the wall.

"Delightful," Pell said, poking the desk. "We can get all the papers out of the dining room. And this phone—keeping it. It's history!"

DH grinned. "Your grandchildren will think it's some alien device. Maybe a relic from another world."

Pell pretended not to feel the comment about grandchildren and turned to look at DH. "Speaking of phones from this century, how do we communicate? Just cell phones? Do you have Wi-Fi on board?"

DH said, "No, but Ned was working on that before he left. I'll get in touch with Daniel Tobey. He runs Singing Wire Telecom out of the tribal lands. See what he says."

Outside on the gravel, DH gestured toward the diesel and septic tanks, water hoses, and yellow yard engine.

"We use that little yard engine to roll over to the maintenance station. Used to dump straight on the tracks back in the day," he said. "A few miles out of town, no one minded. Different times."

Pell laughed lightly. "Let's keep that to ourselves. I have a feeling the PR Director might not find it funny."

Finally, they inspected the generator and then the coupler at the front of the Pullman. The knuckle coupler jutted like a giant metal hand, fingers curled.

"Railroads shake hands and lock knuckles," DH said.

Pell pressed her palm to the cold steel. "I get the knuckles—but the handshake?"

DH pointed to the brake air hose. The ends resembled a perfect clasp.

"Hook these up for air to the brakes. That 'pfft' you hear when cars separate? That's the handshake letting go."

For a little while longer, they let themselves be carried by the rhythm of discovery, trading jokes and plans like co-conspirators. The Pullman became their whole world, crowding out the darker worries waiting beyond its steel walls. Once, the memory of Ned's midnight knock pressed at the edge of the moment; Pell let it pass, just for now.

By the time they returned to the back of the car, the fog was lifting. The Pullman loomed in front of them, battered, quirky, and full of surprises. Pell drew her jacket tighter and studied its scarred flank, the peeling paint, the streaked windows. It looked like her, she thought—worn down by time but not finished yet after all. The car had one more journey in it. Pell hoped she did too.

The next morning, Pell returned to the Pullman car and found DH perched on the rear platform, fingers drumming against the cold steel railing. The mid-morning air carried the sharp tang of brackish water mixed with diesel fumes from the yard engine, a smell that always reminded him of years spent on the rails.

"Morning. I'll call Singing Wire today," DH said, pulling out his phone and checking the time. "See if we can get Wi-Fi humming before this beauty leaves the yard."

"Wi-Fi on a hundred-year-old Pullman," Pell said. "Nothing says modern luxury like a hotspot in a historic car." She ran her fingers along the scratched metal of the coupler, feeling the grooves worn smooth by decades of use.

"I located Cassiday Sail and Yacht online last night. They list upholstery and foam in their inventory and can cut mattresses to fit. I'll run over there as soon as we hear from Alan Granger."

Pell looked around, disliking the feeling of wasting a beautiful day waiting for Granger's call.

"Are you up for an early lunch?"

DH nodded. "Yeah. Plenty of stuff in the fridge. I'm on hold. I think this might take a while."

Pell nodded, climbed up to the platform and headed for the kitchen. DH waited until she was out of hearing range then dialed another number.

"Ned?" he asked, leaning against the railing, one eye on the platform door. His voice was low, cautious.

"Yeah, it's me DH." came the muffled reply. "I'm still laying low on the reservation. Daniel's got me staying at his ranch in the bunkhouse. Catch me up."

DH's gaze flicked toward the door. He could see Pell carrying things to the dining room.

"Your Aunt is here. She met with the board to get permission to use the Pullman. Pretty good plan to get her foot in, but we haven't heard back yet. Pell thinks it will probably be a go. She's playing the rich old excentric and thinks they bought it."

His eyes narrowed. "Ned, about Pell... I can tell she's no dummy. But she's... too transparent. I worry she might slip."

Ned's voice softened, imperceptibly. "She can be trusted, but you still need to be careful. For my safety and yours too." DH exhaled, the tension in his shoulders only partially easing.

Ned continued, "I didn't have a chance to tell you but Granger's on our side. He's been my inside man on the board. He has some information for me. We can meet at the far end of the reservation station crossing next run south. Tell Operations you're stopping to get rock off the track or something."

Pell was approaching the door. DH said, "Got it" and broke the connection just as she poked her head out the door.

"Lunch is served."

"Good. The damn Singing Wire hold timed out on me. I'll try again later."

Over lunch, DH asked Pell her plan for the day.

She said, "I don't really know since we're in a waiting game at this point. What is there to see or do around here?"

DH thought for a minute.

"Not really a tourist destination, but there is an old lighthouse people like to visit. Good fishing out there too."

Pell caught the hint about fishing. "I could look at a lighthouse. But I'm not much for fishing. How about you catch fish, and I take a blanket and lounge chair from the hotel and catch up on my reading?"

DH nodded. "It's a plan."

They crunched across the gravel yard to where DH's faded blue pickup was waiting. To Pell's surprise, it started right up.

"That's impressive. How old is this workhorse?"

"About twenty-five. I take care of my machines and then they take care of me."

As they drove slowly out of the railyard, Pell opened a window and let the wind tousle her hair. They stopped at the hotel and Pell dashed in to get her book and a blanket. She threw that into the truck bed, then borrowed a lounge chair from beside the modest pool, careful to avoid the desk clerk's eye.

Pell thought the lighthouse looked like, well, a lighthouse. A short drive further, DH pulled into a parking spot sheltered by a low dune, grabbed his tackle and rod from the truck, and helped Pell with her chair. They walked down a sandy path through the dune. There, the Atlantic spread before them, gently tossing low waves, smoothing over and pulling away from a small beach.

Pell wrapped herself in the hotel blanket and watched as DH cast into the waves, flicking his wrist just so. The gentle boom and hiss of the moving water lulled her as gulls called and circled above. Just for a moment, it felt like a different life. One where Ned wasn't in trouble with his board scheming against him. One where she felt strong. Despite herself, Pell drifted into a light sleep, book in hand.

For Pell's sake, DH looked more relaxed than he felt as he fished. He noticed she looked exhausted today. Probably to be expected after travel, the big presentation, worry about her nephew. His eyes kept scanning the beach. About a hundred yards away, he caught a glimpse of a movement behind a stand of sea oats and tensed. A deer stepped shyly through the brush. DH relaxed but the micro-uncertainty reminded him: Enemies were still out there, unseen, and any mistake could be dangerous.

Hours passed in small rituals: untangling his line, changing bait. Pell woke and strolled the beach, examining fragments of glass and interesting shells. Even amid this calm, the tension never fully left, and Pell jumped when her phone buzzed in her pocket. Granger's brisk, professional voice cut through the respite of the lazy afternoon.

Mrs. Mellors? Its Alan Granger. I have the contract we discussed earlier this week. It's a go, if you agree to the terms. I think you'll be pleased. Are you available to go over it before you leave?"

Pell said, "That's good news and yes, I can meet you at your office tomorrow. What time works?"

"The board would like me to have a look at the Pullman. Can we meet there at ten?"

"Of course. I'll meet you in the railyard office at ten."

DH watched as Pell ended the call and began reeling in his empty line. It was time to get back to reality.

Chapter Four
The Contract

Penelope Mellors—Pell Mell, as her sister Veronica nicknamed her long ago—sat upright in the stiff-backed chair in the railyard office, trying not to sneeze. The place smelled of diesel and dust, old paper, and coffee gone bitter in its pot. Behind the desk sat the yardmaster, who had the dubious honor of being both witness and gatekeeper to whatever was about to unfold. He had been sorting invoices until a visitor arrived—Alan Granger, business casual in khakis and a checked shirt, his tie absent but his briefcase firmly in hand.

The yardmaster's jaw dropped. "Mr. Granger?"

Granger gave a nod, faintly amused at the man's expression.

"You—you don't usually come down here," the yardmaster stammered. "Not yourself, I mean. We usually get a memo, or a lawyer, or—"

"Thought I'd see the situation in person," Granger replied, breezy but not unkind. He had the relaxed confidence of a man who generally expected things to go his way.

The yardmaster blinked, glancing from Granger to Pell. The juxtaposition clearly rattled him: Granger, the board member; Pell, the eccentric woman who had shown up insisting she'd restore a decrepit Pullman out of sheer affection. His eyes narrowed. Was management spying on the yard? Did they know about the union talk?

"Don't mind him," Pell said. "He's only impressed that a man of such lofty station as yourself should descend into this humble realm."

The yardmaster gave a nervous laugh that sounded more like a hiccup. Granger chuckled outright.

"Well," he said, extending a hand to help Pell up. "Shall we get started?"

Pell led him across the yard to the siding where the Pullman sat in the sun, looking as drab as ever. Dead Head—DH—stood by the steps, wiping his palms on his jeans before extending one to Granger. The two men clasped hands firmly.

"Good to see you, Alan," DH said.

"And you," Granger replied warmly. "Looks like you're coming back to yourself."

Pell observed with interest. There was genuine affection in that handshake, an ease she hadn't seen in DH with anyone else. He had been tentative, wary, almost bashful since she'd met him. Now, with Granger, he seemed relieved to have an ally, or at least a history.

Still, something in Granger's eyes unsettled her and she remembered his hard words during the meeting with the board. A flicker quickly smoothed over. He was sleek, well-kept. Though dressed casually, Pell knew enough to spot expensive when she saw it. What was his motive really, beyond saving his own skin? Ned wanted to save his family's legacy. She loved him and wanted that for him too and really, had nothing to lose at this point. At first, DH just seemed to be along for the ride, but Pell was beginning to see that he was proud of what he and the men he had worked with all these years had built with their strength and sweat and skill. But Granger? Would he really risk much? In a pinch, could he turn? She needed to be sure of him. And wasn't.

"I heard from Ned," DH said. "He mentioned you had news."

Pell's eyes widened and she interrupted. "You heard from Ned? When were you going to tell me? Is he all right?"

DH nodded. "Yes, he's fine. I wanted to know the board's reaction first."

Granger's eyes flicked to Pell, then back. "I understand you're holding Ned's stock now."

Pell shot DH a sharp look, startled again that Granger knew that. DH said simply, "You can trust Alan."

Exasperation prickled at her. She thought she and DH had moved beyond this kind of half-truth.

But can I trust you, DH? "Look, both of you—I need to know whatever you know, when you know it. Ned is my nephew. I can't be of any use to him if I don't really know what's going on."

DH looked down at his boots, but Granger nodded. "You deserve to know what's happening with the railroad. But first things first—we need to settle the contract on this car. Otherwise, we don't have the cover we need to expose the board."

He tapped the briefcase. The metal clasp clicked open with an oddly ceremonial air.

Pell gestured toward the Pullman. "Shall we?"

Inside, the Pullman smelled faintly of lemon and soap—progress already from its previous mustiness. They gathered in the sunlit dining room. Granger laid out a crisp packet of papers on the polished table.

"I'll read these," Pell said briskly, already drawing the sheaf toward her. "Why don't you let DH give you the tour? I find concentration easier without an audience."

Granger grinned. "Fair enough. Lead on, old friend."

The two men disappeared down the corridor. Pell could hear their voices receding—Granger's smooth baritone, DH's dry replies—as she adjusted her glasses and began reading.

The contract itself was straightforward: permission granted to use and restore the Pullman, responsibilities outlined in detail. She read every clause, making notes in the margins with her fountain pen. Nothing seemed amiss—until she reached the section on expenses.

Her brows rose. The Cassiday Company—one of the holding entities supposedly managing "capital improvements"—would pay for all repairs and operations, provided Pell submitted receipts monthly.

She lowered the papers and stared into the middle distance. That was odd. She had expected to shoulder the costs herself. She had even made it plain she was willing. Why would the company offer to fund what she knew would be a very expensive proposition?

When the tour concluded, the three reconvened in the dining room.

"Well," Pell said, tapping the document, "it all looks in order. However—this clause. I had offered to pay, yet here it says Cassiday will cover everything. I confess I'm confused."

Granger opened his briefcase once more and withdrew a manila envelope, thick with papers. He slid it toward her.

"That," he said, "is exactly why I'm here. I need you to get these papers to Ned. They're evidence of part of the fraud someone, or maybe several someones, on the board have been pulling. These are receipts for capital projects that were supposedly executed—what actually got spent versus what the company claimed."

DH frowned, his voice a low growl. "That explains a lot. Letting the rolling stock and track decay, the freeze on wages and crossing fees to the tribe—none of it has been improved for years, no matter how often the safety officer reports it. It's gotten dangerous. That's what started the union talk."

Pell opened the envelope's flap. Inside were invoices, bills, and notes scrawled in different hands. The numbers told a tale at once dull and shocking: small repairs billed as major overhauls, replacement parts marked up threefold, projects that had never gotten started at all.

"They're going to use your Pullman restoration and operation as another capital project to pump money out of," Granger explained. "For example, they'll pay a painting crew two thousand for a job, then claim it cost twenty. The rest gets written off—or siphoned into whatever pocket they choose. Every so-called improvement is the same. My guess is payments are being funneled through Cassiday Company to add another layer of deniability. And of course, Cassiday takes its cut."

Pell frowned. "If I sign this contract, won't DH and I be vulnerable to charges when this reaches the authorities?"

Granger shook his head. "You and DH are just contractors on this project. However, I won't lie. One sticky part is that you're also holding Ned's stock." He sighed. "And the bigger problem is the other board members have Ned and me in a trap."

"What kind of trap?"

He produced a second envelope. "Board meeting minutes. They show all of us present when the Capital Improvement Plan was agreed upon, along with approvals of inflated accounting reports. Ned, me, everyone listed as present. Minutes of meetings that never happened. If this comes out, we're implicated right alongside the real culprits. It was a clever move. Haskell was only too happy to make sure I had copies to make that point.

Pell pressed her lips together. Ned had suspected rot; now Pell was seeing how far its roots spread. And how deeply it ensnared even men like Granger—decent enough, but not immune. He was already shading things to protect himself. She felt the faintest tremor in her hand and clenched it around the pen to steady herself.

"Then we must think this through carefully," she murmured.

"Yes," Granger agreed. "Ned wants these exposed at the right time. For now, we keep our heads down."

Pell looked at DH and shrugged. "As a wise man observed only yesterday, 'What's life without a little risk? What the hell. I wasn't doing much anyway.'"

She signed the contract with a flourish of her pen, though she felt the weight of the moment heavy as a stone.

"Well," DH said, relief in his voice, "at least that's settled. If we get started right now, the Pullman could be ready for the next southbound trip."

Granger nodded, then hesitated. "One more thing. Marissa Sadler insists on a christening ceremony before the maiden voyage, as she is calling it. She also wants to ride with you for the first few stops."

Pell blinked. "The pretty young woman from the meeting? In the cranberry suit?"

"That's her," Granger said. "Our Director of Public Relations. Don't underestimate her. Everything she hears goes straight to the bald fellow's ear. He's her boyfriend."

Pell nearly dropped her pen. "Her boyfriend? He was positively rude to her!"

"Yeah," Granger said wryly. "It's one of those relationships. But Baldy—Charles Haskell, our CFO and now "Interim CEO" since Ned left—is clever. Possibly dangerous. Ned suspects he's the mastermind behind most of the fraud. We haven't even begun to untangle what he's doing with the stock.

"Then I shall treat Miss Sadler like the daughter I never had," Pell declared. "She will ride in comfort until the stop before Tobewanaki, where she can be met by a company car and returned to headquarters triumphant. That way she sees enough to gossip, but not so much as to do damage. The fact that she can be trusted to report to Baldy—I mean, Haskell— is almost as good as having her on our little team. Maybe better."

Granger allowed himself a smile. "Clever yourself, I see. All right, then—you two had better get to work."

He shook hands again, this time with both Pell and DH, and departed the car with the same casual confidence with which he'd arrived.

Silence settled in, filled only by the hum of distant locomotives and the creak of the old Pullman on its tracks. Pell leaned back in her chair.

"Well, DH," she said softly, "we have a contract, a conspiracy, and a spy for a passenger. And a friend who may not be a friend when the fire gets too hot."

DH frowned. "Alan? No, he's solid."

She gave him a measured look. "Solid enough until it's his neck on the line. Call it woman's intuition, but I sense he likes his life far too much to throw it away for a principle."

DH started to argue, then stopped. He thought of the quick glance Granger had given the door, of the sigh when the fake minutes appeared. "All right," he said reluctantly. "I'll be cautious."

Pell nodded and smiled, but the gesture was a cover. A pulse of weakness had throbbed through her chest. She breathed slowly, pushed it down, unwilling to let DH see. She felt not fear but frustration with her body. She was not at her sharpest, and the people arrayed against them were professionals, practiced in fraud and deceit. She could not afford to be the weak link—not with Ned's future at stake, not with DH's fragile revival hanging on this work.

The feeling subsided and they gathered their notes, lists, and contacts: mattresses to order, linens to source, painters to hire, cleaners to schedule, and a safe to buy. Pell had scribbled errands in her tidy hand; DH added names of railyard friends who could help. Together they compiled the day's campaign against mildew, grime, and rust.

But as they stepped off the car into the bright afternoon, Pell felt no lift in her spirits. The Pullman was no longer merely her project, nor even a contested prize. It had become one small front in a much larger war. And she knew, with a chill certainty, that this was not something she could fix with a toy train car or DH could repair like a vintage engine.

If they were to stand a chance, they would need help. The thought was sobering—and terrifying.

Chapter Five
The Christening

Pell and DH stood side by side, letting the late afternoon sun wash over them as they admired the Pullman. Its freshly painted exterior gleamed, deep maroon panels catching the light, the letters *North-South Pulp and Paper Railroad* in gold leaf sharp, proud, and unyielding against the siding. Brass fittings glimmered, as if the car had been born anew.

DH's eyes lingered on every detail, wide with awe. Pell studied him and thought he looked like a new father, overwhelmed by a miracle that had taken shape in his own hands. She allowed herself a private smile. Even with everything hanging over their heads—boardroom treachery, fraud, and her own unspoken fragility—she felt the pure delight of accomplishment.

The last few days had been an exhausting but exhilarating whirlwind. Scaffolding framed the car on every side, painters moving with almost balletic precision, though occasionally losing balance and sending tiny clouds of dust across the panels. Inside, a fire-and-water restoration team steamed carpets untouched for fifty years. At one point, Pell caught a worker gingerly lifting a rug only to reveal a perfectly flattened mouse. Professional cleaners scrubbed every nook, removing decades of grime, grease, and something that smelled vaguely of forgotten cigars.

DH supervised it all like a general commanding an elite army, moving smoothly between contractors, lifting a hand at the exact moment a painter leaned too far over a ladder. Pell silently narrated his heroics like a sports commentator: *"And here comes Dead Head, narrowly avoiding a collision with a bucket of paint! Crowd goes wild!"* She bit back a laugh but admired him all the same. Even the gods of rail seemed to smile on them, as three days of uninterrupted sunshine blessed their work.

Pell's own contributions were less heroic but necessary: ferrying people from the railyard office, running errands for forgotten supplies, and handling Cassiday's relentless upselling. She endured it with wry amusement. *Yes, I do need a matching set of hand-polished silver butter knives for a car with six people, thank you very much.*

Still, the dishware that arrived was impeccable: six place settings, gleaming cutlery, crystal glasses that caught the sunlight and threw tiny rainbows across the floorboards. She tucked them neatly into the built-in dining room cabinet, a contrast to the once-chaotic paperwork now stowed in the secretary's cubby.

Just as she was going to sit down for a moment, Pell's phone buzzed. The yardmaster's name flashed.

"Marissa is at the desk," he said. "She's ready to be escorted to the car."

Pell and DH exchanged a glance that was equal parts curiosity and apprehension. Pell arched one eyebrow. *Here comes our first social test,* she thought. She gave a small nod to DH and set off toward the office.

Marissa Sadler appeared like a sparkling country music star: jeans embroidered with rhinestones, a chambray shirt in delicate cranberry, and boots that could have bought a modest house. Pell's grin widened as she practically skipped to meet her.

"Well!" Pell exclaimed, throwing open her arms. "What an honor! You are the very first visitor to the completed Pullman!"

Marissa's lips curved into a practiced smile, but her eyes sparkled. "I can't wait to see it—and to tell you all about the christening tomorrow." As they walked she added, "Local news will be there, and the company is filming a documentary for the stockholders' meeting."

"Oh, you've been busy. Here we are." Pell swept her arm toward the Pullman stairs. DH emerged, smiling as he helped Marissa aboard and opened the platform door for her.

Pell followed, regarding the car's interior with fresh eyes: polished brass, restored carpeting, and a dining room set with flawless dishes and glasses.

Marissa gushed, "It's adorable! Just like the little car you showed us, except bigger." As instructed by Pell earlier, DH only nodded and smiled.

"I'm so glad you like it," Pell said, taking Marissa's elbow. "Now this is your compartment—the Marissa Suite."

Marissa pulled the door open. The berth was folded down. Silk sheets glimmered in the sun, fresh flowers adorned the table, chocolates waited on a silver tray, and a bottle of chilled white wine promised relaxation.

"It's all so clever and vintage. I feel like I'm starring in a black-and-white movie."

"That's the idea," Pell said with a light laugh. "Step inside—you're traveling backward in style."

Marissa paused, thoughtful. "That's good. We'll work that into the script tomorrow."

DH muttered something about the yard engine needing attention and slipped away. Pell shot him a pointed *thanks a lot* glance; he disappeared, sheepish, leaving her alone with Marissa.

After a quick look at the kitchen, the two women settled into a velvet couch in the salon. Sun poured through the windows, gilding the space. Pell offered coffee and sliced cake.

"Or would you rather have that wine from your room?"

"Oh yes, let's have the wine."

Pell followed her back down the passageway, stopping to retrieve two glasses from the cabinet.

Once resettled with wine in hand, Pell asked, "Why only a few stops? You're welcome to go as far as you like."

Marissa shrugged. "I have to get back to organize for the documentary tomorrow and Charles, I mean Mr. Haskell, prefers to keep me within sight." She smirked faintly, a touch of rebellion in her tone.

Pell's leg rested lightly over the hidden compartment in the floor, where the new safe held contracts and evidence of the board's malfeasance. Pleasure and danger, sharing the same room.

The wine loosened conversation. Pell shared stories about her late husband George: domineering, yes, but marvelous in ways only she could articulate. Marissa listened intently, then revealed fragments of her own life: a mother gone too soon, a career built on work, charm and persuasion, and the constant balancing act with powerful men. Pell offered reassurance, her voice softening. Marissa wasn't a bad person—just naïve and in over her head.

"Any mother would be proud of you," Pell said. "You can consider me a sort of aunt, if it helps."

Marissa's lips quivered slightly, one careful tear sliding down her cheek. Pell took the little Pullman car from its shelf and handed it to her.

"Here. This should be yours. I can see you appreciate the old gal, and I want you to have it."

Marissa's fingers lingered on the brass fittings, eyes glistening. Pell was privately pleased; she meant it. Yes, she was playing a part, but not everything had to be insincere.

Filming began early the next morning, well before the press arrived. Marissa had cast a sexy young actress as Pell and a ridiculously handsome actor as DH. Pell wondered what Marissa thought they had been doing on the Pullman. The two real-life counterparts stood off to the side, trying not to laugh as the actors earnestly declared the Pullman "a time machine linking the glory of the past with the triumphs of tomorrow." Corporate mythology at its most florid.

Pell's phone buzzed. She and DH guided the press into the yard near the Pullman in their van, antenna sprouting from the roof. It was time for the christening, the pièce de resistance. As local broadcaster

Maynard Thomas narrated, Marissa—back in her signature cranberry suit—stood on the Pullman's platform and swung hard. The bottle refused to break. Again. And again. Finally, it shattered, drenching Marissa in a glittering cascade of wine. She laughed harder than anyone, a full-bodied laugh that washed over the crowd and guaranteed good footage for the evening news.

When the crews departed, Marissa changed back to her rhinestone jeans, and she and Pell returned to the salon and sipped the last of the coffee.

Outside, DH hooked the yard engine to the Pullman, readying it to be pulled onto the main line and attached to the end of the pulp cars and the North-South engine for the trip south.

Slowly, the Pullman rolled forward after decades of stillness. Pell's pulse quickened—not with fear, but with the electric thrill of work realized, a dream set into motion. The Pullman was alive again. And in a way, so was she.

By evening, Marissa and the last of the crew had filed out, leaving a quiet that felt almost sacred. Pell lingered in the salon while DH went to check the couplings one final time. She followed halfway, then stopped, realizing that for the first time she would be spending a night inside her restored Pullman—and not alone.

In her compartment, Pell changed into flannel robe and pajamas and pulled down the berth. Normally she felt cozy in the compact spaces of the car, yet tonight that closeness made her chest tighten. She returned to the salon as DH came back, casual as ever, but she noticed a small hesitation in his gait—as if he, too, were aware of the new intimacy.

It was not sexual; there was no suggestion of impropriety. It was the quiet recalibration of two longtime loners learning to share space.

"Dinner?" DH offered.

Pell shook her head, smiling. "No, I'm fine. Just winding down. It's been a good day, but I'm still a little wired."

DH glanced toward the cabinet. "There's about half a glass left in that bottle you and Marissa shared. Care to finish it?"

"Perfect idea."

"Sit still—I'll bring it."

He returned with the wine, a glass, and an O'Doul's beer.

"Thank you," Pell said. She raised her glass. "Not to be sentimental, but we owe ourselves a toast—to us, and what we've pulled off."

DH leaned in, touching his bottle to her glass.

"To you—for bringing this old car, and me, back to life. And may we stay the hell out of jail."

"I'll definitely drink to that."

They sat in companionable silence a while longer, the weight of the day settling gently.

Finally, Pell stood. "I'm looking forward to trying my new berth. Good night, DH."

"Sleep well," he said.

Pell offered a soft smile. "I will—knowing the Pullman's ready, and you're here."

Back in her berth, the train's creaks and sighs became a lullaby. Outside, the moonlight gleamed on the Pullman's golden lettering. Pell closed her eyes, savoring the sensation of hope: the car alive, a start on helping Ned, and the quiet companionship of a man who had become indispensable without ceremony.

In the morning, she would rise to the first full day of the maiden voyage, with cameras, Marissa—Charles's eyes and ears aboard, though still expecting to be treated like a chum—and all the chaos that would bring. But tonight, there was only the Pullman, the soft glow of the sconces in the passageway, and the steady presence of DH. A small, perfect victory. Pell allowed herself to breathe it in.

Chapter Six
Southbound!

The Pullman hummed along the rails, a steady beat vibrating through its polished floors. Pell leaned against the cool sill of the salon window, eyes half-closed, letting the rhythm settle her nerves. The sun poured in, highlighting the freshly varnished wood, the gleam of the brass handles, the newly brightened pattern of the salon's Persian rug. Outside, the landscape blurred into green and gold, the summer sun painting each ridge and valley in molten color.

Documentary filming done, Marissa was free to enjoy the trip. She sat opposite Pell, hands folded delicately on her lap, porcelain cup of coffee steaming beside her. She appeared composed, polished, perfectly coiffed, but Pell could sense the tension beneath the veneer. Every now and then, Marissa's gaze strayed to the passing terrain, wide-eyed at heights and curves, betraying her mixture of excitement and apprehension.

DH was up front with the engineer, an old friend. Pell imagined him standing steady, eyes sharp, watching the track ahead as the engineer coaxed the old engine along. The Pullman rolled smoothly. It took Pell and Marissa a short while to get used to walking down the passageway while in motion, but they soon got their "sea legs" established.

The first bridge of the route came into view, steel girders arching high above a sparkling river far below. Pell's stomach fluttered at the height. She saw Marissa stiffen across from her.

"It's terrifying," Marissa whispered, her fingers gripping the armrest. "I've never been this high up before."

Pell recalled DH's comment that the tracks had not been well maintained for some time. She hoped that did not include the bridges. Attempting a reassuring smile, she said, "It's amazing, isn't it?"

Marissa nodded, eyes wide, and for a moment, neither spoke, absorbed in the scene: white-capped water, glinting sunlight, and the sense of being suspended above it all in a machine both elegant and powerful.

An hour later, the second bridge was even higher. Pell felt a thrill at the sight of the river, now a silver thread far below. The train swayed slightly as they crossed, the wheels singing on steel. Marissa, looking green, turned away from the window. Pell, feigning calm, leaned a hand lightly on the polished window-sill, a quiet counterbalance to the height-induced flutter in her chest.

Soon, the first mountain grade rose ahead, the Pullman tilting as the engine put its shoulder into the climb. On the downslope, trees outside became a blur, sunlight dappling through thick leaves. The rhythm of the wheels quickened, the diesel engine hissing and chuffing, yet steady and confident under the engineer's hand. Pell marveled at the sheer power, imagining the days when coal and steam worked together in perfect, if smokey, harmony.

Miles passed before the route's one tunnel yawned before them, a black maw in the grey rock mountain. As darkness swallowed the view, Marissa and Pell saw themselves reflected back in the Pullman's windows. Beneath them, iron wheels sang loudly on the rails, amplified and echoing against the tunnel's walls. Pell was surprised by the sudden wash of sun into the salon as the train emerged into light, the mountain receding behind them.

The women were cleaning up their lunch leftovers when the first stop appeared: a quaint industrial siding serving the paper factory. Red brick buildings with peeling paint, steel-framed windows, and soot-streaked smokestacks stretched beside the track. Despite the age and utilitarian design, there was an unintentional charm to the busy place. Workers in coveralls moved with practiced efficiency, offloading and guiding large carts of raw pulp from the rail cars into the building. The air smelled faintly of resin, wet paper, and diesel.

Marissa's eyes brightened when she spotted her promised limousine waiting. Pell helped her carry her bags and the small Pullman gift, safely boxed. She boarded the limo and Pell called, "I hope you'll ride again soon," as the long car started forward. Marissa looked back, waving and smiling, their bond sealed with this small, human gesture.

After the limo disappeared down the road, Pell returned to the Pullman. She drifted toward Marissa's compartment, intending to tidy it. The berth was down, the coffee service was still on its tray, perfume lingered faintly in the air. As Pell reached to straighten the nightstand, her eye caught something on the floor in the corner.

She froze. A small, black object with a stubby antenna lay there, half hidden in the shadow where the rug didn't quite meet the wall.

Her pulse quickened as she bent to pick it up. Pell's first thought was disbelief—had she imagined it? No. The cheap plastic and stubby antenna left no doubt. A listening device.

The shock was sharp, personal. It confirmed Marissa had meant to betray her. Pell shook her head. Marissa had probably dropped it while gathering her bags. Careless, nervous, not an adept spy. The thought gave no comfort. If anything, it made the sting worse.

Pell's mind flared with rapid-fire paranoia. What had it heard? She replayed snippets of conversation in her head: "Maybe we can get this company on its feet," "Charles is always one step ahead," "DH and the engineer are handling the grade like a pro." Each line, harmless moments before, now felt like ammunition in Charles's hands.

She remembered Marissa's gestures, her laughter, the way she'd fussed with the coffee cups—small humanizing touches that now seemed tinged with betrayal. Pell felt a mix of pity and anger, a cocktail of emotions she could barely process.

Pell's first instinct was to crush the bug under her heel. The satisfaction would be immediate. But she forced herself to be still. Destroying it could alert Charles. Better to let him believe she and DH were unaware. That way, she held the stronger card: she knew he was listening; he didn't know she knew. Even if she had to pretend ignorance, she would have the advantage.

Pell turned the object in her hand, feeling its plastic edges, so small for the weight of the insult it carried. Then, with a tight jaw, she set it back exactly where she'd found it, antenna angled toward the room.

Her thoughts flicked to DH. Alone in her compartment, she realized how few allies she had. Marissa compromised and careless. DH up front, competent but distant. Ned, confined to Tobewanaki lands for his own safety.

Charles, though invisible was encroaching. Every conversation, every movement could now carry consequences. The Pullman, rolling freely over mountains and bridges, had become a kind of chessboard, and she was both player and piece.

Pell immediately texted DH.

"Listening device in Marissa's compartment. Might be more. Watch what you say."

Seconds later, his dry reply buzzed back: "10-4. Mouth shut. Eyes open. Telling Ned." The simple code of trust was comforting, yet fragile—she knew she would need more than this to stay ahead.

Standing alone in the compartment, Pell looked around with fresh eyes. The walls seemed thinner, the silence less private. She noticed the thrum and creak of the train over the rails, the subtle scent of Marissa's perfume lingering in the air, the soft tick of a brass clock echoing in the quiet. Every detail seemed amplified now, a reminder that she was being observed.

Beneath the rush of hurt and paranoia, Pell's resolve began to harden. She would move carefully, speak deliberately, and plan her next steps. If Charles wanted to put his ears into her Pullman, he would find she could speak louder, and more cleverly, than he had bargained for. Allies would be essential, strategy even more so. A new game had begun, and she intended to be ready.

# Chapter Seven
Rocks on the Track

The Pullman rolled onward, entering Tobewanaki territory. A rough-hewn wooden sign marked the border, painted letters stark against the timber. Pell's eyes swept over small clusters of homes: neat, well-kept houses, trailers, and more modest shacks, all surrounded by cars and trucks in various states. Flowerpots brightened windowsills, shutters bore fresh paint, and small gardens hinted at pride despite limited means. Children waved at the train, some running alongside for a short distance before falling back. The Pullman glided on, graceful and silent except for the drumming of wheels on steel, carrying

Pell and DH into a new landscape, both literally and metaphorically.

At the front of the train, DH's sharp eyes spotted a small pyramid of rocks deliberately placed on the track. The engineer reacted immediately, brakes hissing, wheels screeching as the Pullman slowed. Pell felt the jolt in her chest, the compression of the cars as the train braked, and a long grinding squeal of metal on metal. Her heartbeat quickened, and she found herself pacing the Pullman's passageway, running small circuits to shake the tight knot of unease in her stomach. Breathing hard, she tried to steady herself, reminding herself that DH and the engineer had it under control—but awareness of the threat made her pulse race.

As the train ground to a stop, Pell saw a pickup carrying a contingent of men pull up alongside the train, three more approaching on horseback. Pell emerged onto the platform as one man dismounted, smiling broadly. Pell hurried from the Pullman, wrapping him in a quick hug. Ned. His new beard framed a tanned, matured face, a slouch hat perched casually on his head. Relief surged through her, but her chest tightened with worry—she had discovered Marissa's culpability and wasn't so sure about her health. In that instant, Pell felt like a potential weak link for the first time.

DH's hand briefly waved, and he and Pell held fingers to their lips, motioning the men away from the train to a spot under a nearby shade tree. Pell mouthed, "There's a bug."

Ned, and Daniel and Cliff Tobey nodded. Ned had received DH's warning text. He shook DH's hand vigorously, mouthing words in a stage whisper. "My goodness, Aunt Pell! Just look at the Pullman! She's beautiful!"

Ned pointed toward Daniel Tobey, retired Army Signal Intelligence corpsman, founder of Singing Wire Telecom, and longtime friend. As Pell shook his hand, he drew her close and whispered, "Let's go see about this bug." Pell nodded, anxious but grateful for his calm, steady presence.

Speaking in the clipped tones reserved for track issues, DH peeled off with Cliff Tobey and the rail crew in the pickup to remove the rocks and exchange operational updates. Pell, Daniel, and Ned quietly climbed into the Pullman, stepping silently down the passageway. Pell took Daniel into Marissa's room, pointing out the bug. Pell hummed and muttered to herself as if alone, masking any stray noise.

Next, she and Ned crept into the salon. Pell retrieved Granger's envelope from the hidden safe and handed it to Ned. He winked at her and padded back down the passageway and outside with the envelope.

Pell poked her head into the Marissa compartment. Daniel held the little device up like a spider, confirming it was indeed transmitting. He snapped it off. Pell felt a cold wash of fear at the implications.

They stepped back outside to the shade tree, joining Ned. Daniel held the bug for a moment, examining it, while Pell's mind raced. Her earlier assumptions about Marissa gnawed at her, but she reminded herself that facts were still incomplete. *I can't act on assumptions yet. Not until I know.*

From their vantage point, they could see Cliff, DH, and the rail crew clearing the rocks ahead. Speaking in a normal tone, Daniel confirmed the bug was now off. The conversation turned to strategy: reactivated it and attempt to send false information or destroy it outright. They men decided to crush it, ending its transmission. Ned ground the device under his heel with great satisfaction.

"Even though we killed this bug," Ned said, "Charles, and whoever else is helping him, are suspicious. I might not be able to stay out of sight for much longer."

Pell's chest tightened again. "Can Ned remain here safely, at least for a while longer?"

Daniel shrugged. "Hard to say. Ned is protected on the reservation under tribal law, so long as federal or state authorities respect tribal sovereignty." Pell exhaled, slightly reassured, yet her mind lingered on the possible risks.

Daniel asked, "Are you sure there aren't any more devices in the car? Maybe cameras? Who's been inside?" Pell's stomach flipped. She recounted the crews who had helped ready the car for the maiden voyage. DH had assured her they were friends—or friends of friends—but that was not exactly comforting.

She continued, "Ned, Granger was also in the compartment. He and DH were in every room, together, but still..."

Ned shook his head. "Damn it. I trusted him. I get it. He might be with Charles in this."

She realized that she had assumed Marissa bugged them. Perhaps Charles, or even Granger, had slipped the bug into her belongings. Charles did like to keep tabs on Marissa. If so, this was about his control and jealousy, and not an indication that Ned's attempt to expose the fraud had been discovered. Pell felt guilt but also resolved that she could not let her guard down, no matter what.

Daniel told Pell how to search the car for additional devices, using her cell phone light to reflect off any hidden camera lenses. Pell nodded, realizing the task ahead needed to be meticulous.

Ned's eyes narrowed as Pell quickly summarized the trap they were in, according to the papers he now had. He and Daniel said they would sort through everything and make a plan when there was more time.

Meanwhile, DH and Cliff's crew finished removing the rocks from the tracks. DH and Cliff returned looking grim. While working, he had asked the crew to update him on the status of promised capital improvements. Complaints poured forth: rails were brittle, steel substandard, equipment dangerous.

"Snakehead rose once, derailed a work car," Cliff said. DH shook his head in disgust as he continued. "Ned was there, working beside us. At least someone from management finally sees what we see. Sooner or later—and probably sooner—someone is going to get killed."

They could not linger. Farewells were brief. Daniel Tobey warmly invited Pell to the friendship powwow in late September. DH would fill her in on the details. Pell asked him to please take good care of Ned.

Ned asked Pell to look in on his father in North Carolina and promised to be in touch when she gave the all-clear for communications. The men mounted their horses and returned to the pickup. Ned gave Pell a smile as they rode away from the side of the train. She could not help but be proud of him. And wondered when he learned to ride a horse.

Pell climbed back into the Pullman. DH poked his head in briefly, saying he would catch up with her that evening after they dropped the next pulp delivery and stopped at the North Carolina railyard.

The Pullman train rolled onward, making its final pulp delivery to the newsprint factory. Small boxcars lined up, forklifts whining as they moved pulp into holding bays to be turned into giant rolls of news-print. Pell watched through the window, thinking of how quickly newspapers seemed to be disappearing from the world. At least all seemed well here, for the moment.

By the time they rolled into the North Carolina railyard, it was nearly dark. Sodium lights flickered on, throwing parked freight cars and steel tracks into long orange shadows. Pell donned a light jacket and walked a slow circuit, exploring while DH spoke with the yard crew and arranged service for the Pullman. The yard smelled of creosote and hot metal, punctu-ated by hissing hoses as water and power were con-nected, and tanks were drained.

At last, the engineer signed off and headed home, leaving the yard quiet. Pell caught DH before he boarded the Pullman, telling him she had completed a search for more bugs and cameras with a fine-tooth comb. "As far as I know, we're clear," she said. "But we should still be careful."

Dinner done, the dishes cleared, Pell and DH finally had a moment of quiet in the dining car, sconces throwing a warm glow over the polished wood.

Pell said, "It was so good to see Ned."

DH gave his half smile. "Turned into a cowboy."

She caught DH up on details about her discussion with Ned and Daniel and asked, "What did you find out while you and Cliff were clearing the tracks?"

DH leaned back. "Snakehead. Rails splitting, men hurt, equipment wrecked."

"What's a snakehead? Not the fish, I take it?"

"Ha! Nope. Old track style—thin metal over wood. Warps, rears up, can puncture a car. We didn't have new T-rails in time, so we rigged a temporary strip to get the work truck through. Gave way. Car derailed. Could've been worse. Company should've had the T-rails sent on time."

Pell said, "Thank goodness it wasn't worse. Any more news about the union organizing backlash?"

"They spied," DH said flatly. "Fired those making progress. Safety reports vanished. Raises handed out selectively, and damn few of those. Tribal camaraderie survived, mostly due to Ned's friendship with Daniel. And I've known Cliff since boyhood. Grew up near the reservation. We used to put coins on this track, watch them flatten under the wheels." His voice softened at the memory.

Pell asked about the powwow Daniel had mentioned. DH described the music and food, the circle of drums, dancing into the night, the deep strength of community.

"At the close, they have a friendship dance where everybody—from all the tribes and guests—joins in. I try to come every year."

Pell was amused. "Do you dance?"

"Darn right I do! Rude not to."

After a pause, Pell said she was off to bed to do some reading.

DH nodded. "I'll clean the kitchen. Get coffee ready for morning. Good night."

"Alright," Pell said. Then, after a silence: "I'll be returning to my house in the morning. You'll be on your own again."

He studied her. "You going to make the north run?"

"I have an important appointment," she said carefully. "I'll let you know."

DH didn't press, but Pell felt the weight of his unspoken question as she rose from the table.

Chapter Eight
The Appointment

Pell sat stiffly in the visitor's chair across from Dr. Cummings' desk, her hands folded primly in her lap, though her eyes had other ideas. They wandered over the surface of his desk, lingering over the tidy stacks of folders, the clipped notes neatly arranged, and the fountain pen laid just so, glinting faintly under the fluorescent office lights. She leaned forward slightly, squinting, trying to read the upside-down print on the nearest file. Her own name was on the tab. She resisted the childish urge to flip it around, a small act of self-discipline she didn't entirely understand. There was a tiny flutter of nervousness in her chest—a whisper of anticipation that this particular moment carried more weight than any mundane visit before.

Tests done. Results in. This was the appointment where she would learn what the shadows in her lung really meant. A sterile scent of disinfectant and polished wood filled the air, pressing against her senses as though the room itself waited with bated breath. She glanced at the small clock on the wall, the second hand clicking steadily, as if counting down the inevitable.

Dr. Cummings' head was bent over the folder, the fluorescent lights glancing off the crown of his scalp. A bald spot, not large, but noticeable if one looked. Not old, not young, Pell thought, squinting slightly to confirm her impression. That's good, she told herself. Steady hands, not worn out. Maybe someone with endurance enough to guide her carefully through what lay ahead. Still, a fragile glimmer of optimism remained.

He looked up, and for a moment, his eyes seemed larger behind the thick lenses of his glasses, almost magnified. "Well, Mrs. Mellors—Pell," he corrected himself gently, "how have you been since our last visit?"

"Fine, for the most part," Pell said, tucking a loose strand of hair behind her ear, a habitual gesture she now realized she used whenever she wanted to stall time, to delay reality. "A bit tired, I guess. A few instances of breathlessness." The words tumbled out quickly, unbidden, as if her body needed to release them before they solidified into fear. Then she tried to reel them back, adding, "Could just have been anxiety, I suppose. I've actually been very busy." She offered a small, ironic smile at the absurdity of her own defense. Busy. A convenient mask for uncertainty.

Dr. Cummings nodded slowly, a deliberate, measured gesture that felt simultaneously reassuring and formal. He opened her folder, the pages whispering against each other like cautious confessions.

"Understandable. Well—" he folded his hands over the papers, a deliberate pause that stretched the silence almost unbearably, "as you know, the test results came in. As we suspected, while it is a type of lung cancer, it's slow-growing, much less aggressive than other kinds. The medical name for it, just for the record, is a lung carcinoid tumor."

Pell blinked, the words catching somewhere in her throat. "Tumor is such a horrible word, isn't it?" she asked, voice soft, almost a murmur, as if speaking it aloud might give it too much power.

He nodded, lips pressed together. "It is. But I want to tell you—we have many treatment options now, and far more successes than even a decade ago. In your case, the usual treatment isn't chemotherapy or radiation, but surgery."

"Slow-growing…" Pell repeated, tasting the syllables like bitter tea. "That's… not exactly a huge relief, is it?"

"No," he admitted softly, leaning back slightly in his chair. "It doesn't make it disappear. But it does give us room—time to plan, to manage. Options that won't overwhelm you."

Her voice wavered. "How big is this tumor?"

He adjusted his glasses, pushing them up the bridge of his nose. "About two and a half centimeters."

Pell did a quick mental calculation, converting the abstract into something tangible. "So… about the size of a small hen's egg, then."

"Roughly, yes," he said. His voice carried a measured calm, though she thought she detected the faintest hint of concern beneath the professional tone.

"But I don't feel anything," she protested, frowning slightly as she placed her hands on the arms of the chair. Her fingers dug lightly into the wood as if she could anchor herself against the reality of the news.

"That's one blessing with this diagnosis," Dr. Cummings said, the corners of his mouth lifting in a faint, cautious smile. "It isn't blocking your bronchial tube—at least not yet."

Pell leaned back, letting out a slow exhalation she hadn't realized she'd been clutching. The air around her seemed suddenly lighter, though tinged with the metallic flavor of fear. "So, I'm… I'm sick. But I have time."

"Yes," he said firmly, "time. And we'll use it wisely. I'd like to schedule surgery as soon as possible. After that, we'll set up regular check-ups. Medication if needed. Lifestyle adjustments. I'll keep a close eye on things, and you'll continue living your life."

She nodded, her eyes lifting to the bland ceiling tiles above him. She counted the small grid of squares, as if the constancy of geometry could offer her clarity. Trying to reconcile fear with the faint glimmer of hope, she whispered, "I suppose… I suppose I have decisions to make."

"You do," the doctor said gently, leaning forward just slightly, "and remember—you don't have to make them alone. Support matters."

She forced a small smile. "Support… yes."

Back at home, Pell moved with purpose, throwing open windows and propping doors. The faint, closed-up smell of absence lifted slightly as she swept through the house, dusting, tidying, rearranging. She laughed to herself at how the rooms now seemed cavernous, almost absurdly large. After so much time in the Pullman, the spaces of her own house seemed overbuilt, as if they had been constructed for giants. Funny how quickly the mind and body adjusted.

She missed the rhythmic thrum of train wheels beneath her feet, the constant, comforting pulse that had accompanied so many of her thoughts and decisions. To fill the sudden quiet, she turned on music, letting a cascade of piano notes ripple through the rooms, soft and melancholic. It did little to chase away the weight pressing on her shoulders. The diagnosis clung like a lead shawl.

If she chose surgery, who would she have for support? DH was a friend, yes, but hardly someone she could burden with this. Ned was confined to the reservation for the foreseeable future. Pell frowned at the thought. She had always been healthy, barely a cavity in her lifetime, eating sensibly, walking daily, avoiding reckless risks. And still.

"I guess it's just my turn," she murmured aloud, half-wry, half-resigned. Her voice echoed faintly against the high ceilings of the old house.

Pell took a walk anyway, letting her shoes scrape softly over the uneven pavement, feeling the cool evening air settle on her face. When she returned, she cooked herself a modest dinner, savoring the routine. She pulled out a bottle of wine, stared at it for a long moment, then slid it back into the rack without opening it. It was too early for bed, but she was going there anyway rather than spend any more time with her own thoughts. Tomorrow she would keep her promise to Ned and go see Victor.

The nursing home was small, tucked on a quiet street, inconspicuous except for the sign in front listing its name and status as a facility offering memory care.

Pell signed in at the front desk and asked which room was Victor's. Just inside, residents sat in small groups in lounge chairs, a muted television filling the common room with chatter. The smell of lunch cooking drifted faintly—roast chicken, perhaps carrots—and beneath it all the faint tang of antiseptic. It was not unpleasant, only clinical. The scent that reminded Pell of both sterility and order.

Pell walked down the corridor, heels tapping softly, until she reached Victor's door. It stood ajar, as though awaiting her presence.

Victor was reclined in his chair, eyes clouded, watching television. When he saw her, his entire face brightened, a boyish grin spreading wide.

"Veronica!" he exclaimed, struggling to pull himself upright. "Where have you been? I've been waiting for you."

Pell's heart squeezed as she sat on a chair beside him. "Victor… V is gone. It's me, Pell. Ned asked me to check on you."

Confusion clouded his features, panic flaring. "What are you saying? Where did V go?"

The words stabbed at her. Pell remembered Victor as he had been: sharp, decisive, endlessly devoted to her sister Veronica. She had not realized until this moment how far the disease had taken him from the man he was. She softened her tone, choosing camaraderie over correction. What was the point of dragging him into thoughts that would cause him pain, and just as quickly vanish?

"I'm here, Victor. Just visiting. Thought I'd keep you company a while."

He calmed and asked about Ned soon after. "When's he coming home from college?"

"Soon," Pell said gently, taking his hand. "And he sends his love."

At that Victor nodded, satisfied for a moment, almost as if he were his old self. Pell noted his clothes were neat, his hair trimmed, cheeks freshly shaven. He seemed well cared for. She continued chatting lightly, laughing at small anecdotes, watching a spark of recognition cross his face from time to time.

A little before noon, a nursing aide popped her head in, smiled at him, and he brightened, clearly familiar with her presence.

"Hi Victor! Lunch will be served soon. Are you interested in joining your table in the dining room? I'll walk you down." Victor nodded and rose carefully from his chair.

Pell said, "Victor, looks like you have a lunch appointment. I'll let you get your lunch and will visit again soon."

Then she walked back down the corridor to the front desk where she introduced herself and explained, "Ned Talmadge, Victor's son, is indisposed for now. I'm Victor's sister-in-law. If anything is needed for Victor, please call me."

The drive home left Pell heavy with pity, and anger too—anger at the waste of a man who had once been so vital, now reduced to fragments of himself.

Then the realization came, sharp as a slap: if she gave in to her own despair and self-pity, she would be doing the same with her life. She might not be of wholly sound body, but unlike Victor, her mind remained intact. To waste that would be not only tragic but selfish.

As she pulled into the driveway, Pell's eyes roved over her house. It looked as it always had but somehow, no longer felt like hers. It resembled a set piece, designed for a family long gone, carefully curated and dusted but drained of living purpose. Pell suddenly understood that without realizing it, since George and then John passed, she had been tending a museum, not a home, living a memory, not a life.

Pell breathed deeply, resolve returning. The damn tumor, or something else, might get her, but she would not emotionally curtail her own life in the meantime.

Her phone rang, its sudden shrillness slicing through the quiet like a warning bell. Pell snatched it up.

It was DH. His voice was tight, urgent. "Daniel called from the Tobewanaki clinic. Ned's there. Pretty beaten up, but not critical. He asked for you."

Pell's grip tightened on the receiver. "What's the fastest way to get there?"

"By the time you got a flight and a rental car, the train will already be at the station."

"I'm on my way," Pell said, feeling her chest pulse with determination. "I'll join you on the northbound trip."

Chapter Nine
Fire!

D H reached down and pulled Pell's bags onto the Pullman platform as she climbed aboard.

"Are we ready to roll?" she asked.

"Yep. All fueled up. Just waiting for you."

He followed her inside and leaned against the doorway of her compartment, watching as Pell unloaded her things. There was something different about her. He couldn't quite put his finger on it. Probably just upset about Ned. That was enough.

Pell turned to look at him. "What can you tell me about Ned? What happened?"

"He's healing. Better than you might think by the look of him. Cliff Tobey said a gang of men set fire to the station. He rousted the volunteer firefighters and Ned jumped right in. Helped fight the fire, then fought like a demon when the gang returned and tried to drag him off. The man's got grit."

"I know," Pell murmured, chest tightening. "But that he's hurt like this… I keep thinking it's my fault."

DH's gray eyes met hers. "Don't. You didn't send them. Someone else wanted him out of the way."

Pell closed her eyes, forcing herself to breathe. "Do we know who did it?"

DH shook his head, grim. "I think we can make a damn good guess! The police chief, and the rest of us, are working on getting proof."

"Alright. I know we need to get underway. Go keep watch on the engine. We can catch up later."

As the train rolled north, Pell settled into the salon, surprised it already felt like home. She'd only been gone a few days, but the passing landscape and steady clatter underfoot made her feel back in the stream of life—or at least doing something, which beat sulking around the house, calling it reflection.

By late morning, the Pullman rested on a siding beside the charred ruins of the Tobewanaki station. The North–South engine and freight cars continued northward on schedule, leaving the smoke and ruin behind.

Pell stepped onto the Pullman's platform. The smell of char and ash tinged the air. The station's blackened skeleton leaned against the sky, timbers sagging, a few boards still smoldering.

Pell climbed down as a gray sedan crunched over the gravel and rolled to a stop beside the Pullman. Mimi Tobey—Daniel and Cliff's mother—sat behind the wheel. DH appeared from around the car as she rolled down her window.

She smiled at DH, then extended her hand toward Pell as he introduced them. Her round face, framed by thick salt-and-pepper hair, radiated warmth, though her eyes held quiet authority.

"Pell, please call me Mimi. Climb in, you two. I know you'll want to see Ned right away."

As she put the car in gear, she added, "The train car will be safe here now. And Pell, you'll stay with me. No sense drifting alone where shadows linger."

Pell studied her face. There was no hesitation, only certainty. "I… I'd like that," she said softly, relief creeping in. "Thank you."

Inside the small clinic, DH and Mrs. Tobey took seats in the corner while Pell hurried to Ned's bedside. He lay propped on pillows, face bruised and swollen, but eyes alert. A weak grin tugged at his lips.

"Aunt Pell," he rasped. "Don't start crying on me. Makes a fellow feel worse. But I'm glad you're here."

Her throat caught. She smoothed the blanket at his shoulders. "I'll save my tears for when you're stronger," she said, though her voice wavered.

He reached for her hand. "You should've seen the other guy. Not much left of him now."

Pell managed a smile. "I have no doubt."

The nurse poked her head in. "Five minutes. He needs rest."

"Nah, they just got here," Ned protested. "Aunt Pell, you staying on the Pullman?"

"No, I'm over at Mrs. Tobey's. Mimi's. Safer that way. There's not much left of the station."

"Good. That's good," Ned said, glancing toward Mrs. Tobey with gratitude. "You two have a lot in common."

"Yes," Pell agreed wryly. "These days it mostly entails worrying about you and the rest of the crew. And here I thought I was just going to clean up an old passenger car and look into some accounting malfeasance."

Ned smiled, then winced. "Sorry, Aunt Pell. Looks like the stakes are higher than I guessed." He looked at DH. "Make sure you keep an eye on her."

"I'll use both eyes, brother," DH said.

Pell brushed damp hair from Ned's forehead. "Okay, we should let the nurse do her work. You rest and get your strength back. No more worrying about me. I'll be back later to say goodnight."

He nodded, eyelids fluttering shut. After a few moments, DH touched her elbow and guided her out. "He's breathing steady," he said softly.

Mrs. Tobey's house was small but ringed by flowerbeds and a vegetable garden Pell envied. Chickens strutted through the yard, clucking like gossips. Inside, the air was rich with the scent of venison stew, thick with herbs and root vegetables. A large stone fireplace anchored the living room. On one wall hung a quilt and an elaborate ceremonial dress, bright against the wood.

Pell inhaled deeply. "That smells wonderful."

"Venison stew and fresh-baked bread tonight," Mrs. Tobey said. "I hope you don't mind, I invited the boys and DH for dinner at six. We need to understand what happened and put our heads together."

"That's a wonderful idea," Pell said. "Tell me how I can help."

"First let's get you situated."

She led Pell down a hall lined with family pictures—Daniel and Cliff as children, then young men, one picture including a rail-thin DH. In Daniel and Cliff's old room, Mrs. Tobey had left only a few shelves of handmade drums and flutes but a toybox in the corner spoke of visiting grandchildren.

"Towels and an extra blanket are on the bed," she said. "Rest if you like. Later you can visit Ned again before the clinic closes."

Pell stowed her things and returned to the kitchen. The percolator bubbled on the stove, and Mrs. Tobey was slicing cheese and fruit.

"I thought we might have a bite," she said. "Dinner's nearly done—just need to put the bread in later and set the table. Should I make a pie? I'm feeling ambitious."

"I think a pie would be just right. Let me know what I can do."

"Do you want to take Ned a bowl of stew? I was going to run some over to whoever Cliff has on watch tonight. DH can bring you back for dinner."

"I know Ned would love some home cooking," Pell said, easing into a chair at the small kitchen table. "Thank you."

They nibbled on cheese and fruit as Mrs. Tobey rolled out dough and packed a box with the stew and a thermos of coffee. Pell's eyes drifted to the ceremonial dress and shawl on the wall in the living room.

"They're beautiful," Pell said quietly. "The dress, the drums and flutes in the boy's room too."

Mrs. Tobey smiled. "They're for our dances. You'll see, and hear, them used at the powwow if you come.

Music and movement are how we remember who we are."

"I make things too," Pell offered. "Not serious, just for fun. Miniatures—like trains, dollhouse furniture. Little worlds you can hold in your hand."

Mrs. Tobey looked up with interest. "A patient craft. Another reason Ned speaks of you so fondly."

Conversation drifted. They spoke of raising sons—of Cliff and Daniel, of George and John, now gone, and of Ned, who was all Pell had left.

Mrs. Tobey listened kindly. "I've met Ned many times with Daniel. I like him. He's steady. I'm sorry for your losses."

Pell nodded, throat tight.

"I'm glad for grandchildren from Cliff," Mrs. Tobey went on. "Still, I wish Daniel would find a wife. Maybe at the powwow, same as I did years ago, or by the river where we dammed the water for a swimming hole. It's still there."

Pell smiled. "I thought I'd found a woman good for Ned. But I'm not sure she is what she seems. Her name is Marissa Sadler. PR Director for the railroad." Pell glanced out the window. "Mimi, I could just be paranoid, but I keep seeing the same dark blue pickup drive by. There is a big dog on the passenger seat."

"That's Mr. Tobey. He lives not far." Mimi added, "We're on a break—it's lasted ten years. Cliff says he is just keeping an eye on things, but I think he's keeping tabs on me. And here I am, still matchmaking!"

Laughter softened the air. When the pie was ready for the oven, they set the table together, quietly pleased to have found a kindred soul. Friendship, Pell thought, was harder to come by with age.

As the bread came out golden and fragrant, Mimi said, "Dinner is basically ready. Let's go deliver the stew."

Back at the clinic, two of Cliff's crew sat in a pickup truck outside, keeping watch. Pell felt a surge of gratitude for their silent vigilance as she slipped inside with her basket while Mimi carried dinner to the truck.

Ned's eyes lit when he saw Pell step into his room with her basket.

"Contraband?" he rasped.

"Only the finest," Pell whispered, setting down the steaming bowl and spoon. "Try not to get caught."

Ned steadied the spoon with bruised knuckles but steady fingers. After the first swallow, he sighed. "Ahh—Mrs. Tobey's stew. That woman can cook almost as well as you, Aunt Pell."

Pell chuckled. "She might have me beat. I'm out of practice. But thank you for the diplomacy, Nephew."

She stayed with him until his eyelids drooped again, her hand resting lightly on his arm. Outside, the guards still sat in their truck, eyes scanning the dusk. Tension coiled in Pell's chest. They weren't safe here—not anywhere.

By the time Pell returned with DH, the house was full of warmth—bread cooling on the counter, the pie still fragrant in the oven. Cliff and Daniel arrived just minutes after they did, kicking boots off and lining them up on the porch before stepping inside. Mrs. Tobey ushered them all toward the table, her presence somehow both commanding and comforting.

"Sit, boys. Food's ready, and I won't have us talking business on empty stomachs."

They obeyed with good humor, Daniel sliding his chair with a wince. Pell noticed Cliff seemed fine aside from a split lip. Seen side-by-side, it was clear they were brothers. Both dark-haired and clean-shaven though where Daniel was barrel chested, Cliff was lean and hard. She found herself between DH and Mimi at the long wooden table now crowded with stew, bread, butter, and bowls of greens.

Cliff bowed his head briefly and said, "Thanks for the food, Mama."

The meal began in near silence, the sound of spoons and bread crusts breaking filling the gaps. Hunger softened, talk gradually returned.

"So," Daniel said at last, glancing around the table. "We all know last night wasn't random. Someone wanted that station gone. And maybe Ned too."

Cliff's jaw tightened. "Arson. Assault. They crossed a line. The station wasn't much but the crews did use it, and hoped to run passengers out of it again one day."

DH kept his tone even. "Lines don't mean much to men like that. They'll keep pushing until we push back. This is war."

Cliff said, "Just tell me who's ass to kick and when."

Mimi glanced at him but said nothing. Pell looked from one face to the next, feeling the heat of their anger. "But how can we fight? We think we know who is behind all this but don't have any proof."

"We've got pieces," Daniel said. "The Police Chief's digging. And Cliff has the crews spreading word to keep watch up and down the line. I think we'll see the company visit tomorrow or the next day. Burning the station and roughing up Ned was likely a warning—and an opportunity for more fraud. They'll probably file a giant insurance claim and replace the old station with something small while billing for big."

DH and Cliff sneered. Pell added, "I don't know if Daniel and DH had time to tell everyone, but there was a bug on the Pullman after Alan Granger, then the PR Director, Marissa Sadler, visited. Ned thought Granger was on our side and Marissa might—or might not—be trustworthy. She is connected to the CFO Charles Haskel. Who has now appointed himself CEO by the way. So, if they show up, it's in our favor to keep up the façade that we think they're friends but be careful."

Nods rippled around the table.

Mimi set her fork down gently. "This is more than one family's fight. More than one boy's bruises. What happens to this railroad touches all of us—our work, our homes, our future."

The words settled like stones. No one spoke for a moment.

Finally, Pell said, "It's true. We need a plan. Not just to defend ourselves, but to hold on to what's ours. Otherwise, we'll always be reacting, always a step behind."

Cliff leaned back, folding his arms and smiling. "Spoken like a General."

"Not a General," Pell corrected. "Just someone who has had it. I'm tired of watching people I love getting hurt and for something we all had a part in building being stolen away."

They ate in silence for a moment longer, but the air had changed. A shared resolve flickered, like kindling catching spark.

When the meal ended, Mrs. Tobey cleared the bowls and pressed pie slices into their hands. The men lingered at the hearth until the clock struck nine, then drifted out with promises to stay alert and check in again tomorrow.

❖ ❖ ❖

That night, after they had gone and Pell and Mimi had cleared the kitchen, Pell sank into a chair near the hearth, Mimi in the one across from her. Pell's chest felt heavy, pressed by worry, guilt, and fear.

"You're carrying more than you should," Mrs. Tobey said gently. "More than just worry for the boy."

Pell exhaled, shoulders sagging. "It's not just Ned. It's everyone. DH, the tribe, the men and women all up and down the line—they're all at risk because of me. And I… I don't even know if we can stop it. And, between us, I'm not exactly the picture of health. I'm okay for now but…"

Mimi tilted her head. "You fear being the weak link."

Pell looked up sharply. "How did you—?"

Mimi gave a faint smile. "I've lived long enough to know the signs. The ones who carry the weight yet try to hide it. The ones who suffer in silence, so others won't bear it."

Pell's throat tightened. She closed her eyes, imagining Ned bruised in the clinic, the Pullman beside the burned station, the men she cared for—everyone exposed. "I can't even protect him. We have no plan. Nothing to fight back with. Just… anger, frustration, questions."

Mimi reached across, covering her hand. "Then perhaps the question isn't what you can control, but what is worth controlling."

The words settled like an ember in Pell's chest. She stared into the fire, watching it shift and crackle. "Is it really worth it? To fight the board, expose the fraud? Save a railroad that might fail anyway?"

Mimi did not speak.

The flames leaned, hissed, then flared against the blackened logs. In that stubborn light, a new thought flickered—fragile but insistent. She thought of DH guiding her through the Pullman restoration, of Ned battered but unbroken, of the Tobewanaki people linked to the history of the railroad, and of Victor's legacy to Ned.

"Maybe… maybe it's not about whether it's worth it," she whispered. "Maybe it's about not letting some-one else decide for us. About claiming what's ours before it slips away."

Mimi's eyes glimmered in the firelight. "Then we try. Together."

The Pullman, the burned station, the men she cared for—all of it waited. Pell sat back, chest aching a little but breath steadier, as though the spark had caught hold. They had no map, no clear plan. But somewhere in the ashes, an idea was waiting to be born.

Mimi leaned forward. "We are about the same age. I've been thinking. Do you remember a union movement up in West Virginia, in a town called Weirton? Everyone gave what they could, and they somehow took over a whole steel mill."

Pell sat up straight, eyes gleaming. "Mimi, I do remember that! You are a genius."

The two women sat late into the night, recalling all they could and starting to outline a vision for a path forward.

After some time, Mimi said, "This is good. This is real. Tomorrow we talk with Daniel and perhaps Ned if he is up to it. But now, bed." She rose. "Sleep well, my friend."

Chapter Ten
Bugs

The black limousine rolled up to the ruins of the station as if it were arriving for a ribbon-cutting ceremony rather than a disaster scene. Ash still hung in the air from the fire and the burned timbers gave off a damp, acrid smell. Out of the limo stepped the railroad's insurance man, white hardhat on, clipboard in hand. Behind him, Marissa Sadler emerged in a tailored coat and a pair of sturdy but brightly patterned boots—practical for the cinders beneath her, yet flamboyant enough to make her presence unmistakable.

"Oh my God," she breathed, already lifting her camera. Not a phone—an actual professional rig with shoulder strap and wide lens. She moved with practiced economy, circling the ruins, adjusting aperture and angle. Whatever else could be said about Marissa, she knew what she was doing when it came to filming.

The two yardmen watching the site stiffened at once. They had been leaning against the hood of a pickup, smoking and keeping half an eye on things. The sight of the company car, the company rep, and Marissa—camera already clicking—was enough to set off alarm bells. One of them pulled out his phone and rang Cliff. Cliff, in turn, rang DH. DH rang Pell.

Pell was at Mimi Tobey's house, trying to decide whether her lungs felt like lead from exertion or from dread. When the call came, she bolted upright. "Marissa and the insurance adjuster? Here already?"

"Yep. Black limo. Insurance guy with her," DH said. "They're filming. I'm at the ranch."

"Damn it," Pell muttered. She scrambled for her coat, moved from room to room looking for Mimi. "We'll be right there."

But Pell was too late.

By the time she reached the scorched platform, Marissa was gone. The insurance man, baby-faced, and sweating, answered Pell's question.

"Marissa caught a fleck in her eye," he explained. "Walked to the clinic for treatment. Said she'd be fine. They're patching her up now."

Pell swore under her breath. *Ned.* With a glance at Mimi, she hurried off toward the clinic.

Inside the clinic, the air smelled of disinfectant. Pell caught her breath when she saw Marissa perched beside Ned's bed, her hand clasping his. Her eyes were red from rinsing, but otherwise she looked composed. Ned, pale but grinning faintly, seemed in no hurry to let go of her hand.

"There she is," Marissa said brightly, rising to hug Pell. "I was so worried. And look at him! He's hurt, Pell. Why didn't anyone tell me?"

"I—" Pell's eyes flicked from her nephew's bandaged wrist to the faint, carefully concealed bruise beneath Marissa's makeup.

"What happened to you?" Marissa asked Ned, her tone hovering between concern and mild accusation. "Why didn't you call me?"

Ned squeezed her hand, his smile evasive. "Just a riding accident. I'll be fine."

Pell couldn't miss the energy between them—the way Ned's gaze lingered, the way Marissa tilted her face toward him, soft and eager. *Oh no,* Pell thought grimly. *This could be a new kind of trouble.*

Ned's nurse soon padded in with a tray, briskly shooing them back so she could feed Ned and change his bandages. Relieved to cut the visit short, Pell told Ned she would be back soon and took Marissa's elbow to guide her out.

Back at the burned shell of the station, Mimi stood stiffly beside the young insurance assessor who was checking item off on his clipboard. Pell joined her as Marissa clicked back into professional mode, camera raised to capture the scene.

"The company asked me to record a background piece," she explained with rehearsed brightness. "About how the railroad and the tribe have always had a strong relationship. How the company was ahead of its time—a pioneer in diversity and inclusion. Like a father to the community. Next, it will show the rebuilding of the station. A phoenix rising from the ashes or something like that."

Mrs. Tobey's lips thinned. "That isn't the truth of our relations with the railroad. Not at all."

Marissa faltered, lowering the camera. "I know," she admitted quietly. "But they're insisting I frame it this way for the spring stockholders meeting."

Mimi's face hardened. Without another word, she turned on her heel, her shawl snapping in the breeze as she walked away.

Pell caught Marissa's arm. "Coffee. Now."

They retreated to the Pullman, the salon's sunny warmth and velvet couches a refuge from ash and smoke. Pell poured two cups of coffee and set them down firmly. Marissa adjusted her lens cap, set the camera aside, and cradled the mug in both hands. Her shoulders sagged.

"I know what you're thinking," she said at last. "That I've sold out. That I just parrot what they tell me."

"That is exactly what I'm thinking." Pell slid a notepad across the table, scrawling a line: *May I search your bag?*

Marissa blinked in surprise but nodded. Pell dug quickly, her breath catching when her fingers closed on the small recording device nestled among cosmetics and spare batteries. She twisted it until it cracked, then slammed it on the table.

"You were bugged," Pell spat, her voice rising as she stood. "Again! Do you understand what this means? It was probably Charles' men who hurt Ned, who torched that building outside."

Marissa's eyes widened. She shook her head violently. "No—no, he wouldn't—" Her voice broke, and she covered her face. "I didn't know. I swear, I didn't know."

"I guess you didn't think he'd give you that bruise you're trying to hide either, did you?"

Marissa's hand shot up instinctively to cover her face. "Pell, I need help. I'm going to leave Charles. I'll quit my job."

"Not yet," Pell said, deliberate. "If you leave now, you vanish. Nothing changes."

Pell took a deep breath and resumed her seat. "If you really want to help, stay inside. Get us the proof we need—documents, orders, anything tying Charles and Granger to the fire, to the money he's been bleeding from the company. That's the only way this ends."

Marissa looked up, mascara streaked, expression raw. "You want me to spy on him?"

"I want you to choose," Pell said. "Keep being his mouthpiece—or help us stop him. Don't imagine you can float in the middle. I'll do what I can to protect you, but you'll have to protect yourself too."

Silence thickened. Pell felt the tension pressing against her ribs, the quiet weight of stakes too high to ignore. At last, Marissa drew a long breath and nodded. "I'll do it. I'll get what you need. I've been pretending for months that I still care for him, so how hard can it be to pretend a little longer? And when I come back—you'll believe me."

Pell studied her face. Somewhere in the fragile resolve, she thought she saw a spark of courage. But she did not trust sparks. Not yet.

"All right then. You better get back to your filming. But don't leave us empty-handed."

Marissa drained her coffee, set down the cup with trembling fingers, and stood. "I won't." She gathered her camera and slipped out into the bright afternoon.

Pell remained sitting, staring at the crushed bug on the polished coffee table. Her anger ebbed into unease. Trust was a currency she could not afford to spend freely anymore. But if Marissa truly meant what she said, perhaps they had acquired an unexpected ally. *Or perhaps another knife pointed at our backs.*

Pell startled at a knock on the platform door. Mimi peered around the half-opened door.

"I've come to tell you they have gone."

"Oh, Mimi, come in! I'm so sorry Marissa said that about the film the company wants." Pell quickly caught her up on the ensuing conversation. "She won't be finishing that PR piece anytime soon."

"Good! I hope we can trust her. I also came to tell you Daniel called. Ned is being discharged, and he is coming to pick him up. Daniel and Cliff both think it's safer if he stays at the ranch. The ranch is harder to find than the clinic."

Pell nodded. "Okay. Let's go over there. I want to tell Ned what just happened with Marissa before he goes."

As Mimi and Pell pulled up to the clinic, Daniel rounded the corner. Mimi stayed to update him on the morning's events while Pell went inside.

Ned was up, energized, and dressed in street clothes. "Hi Aunt Pell. They say I'm cleared to go. Daniel is coming. I'll be bunking out at the ranch again."

"Yes, Mimi told me. Ned, I need to tell you I found another bug in Marissa's bag just now. She denies knowing anything about it and promised she'd help us if she can. Apparently her love for Charles has grown cold. It probably has something to do with that black eye she was hiding. But we still have to be careful trusting her."

Ned's brow furrowed. "That's ugly. But if she's turning against him, we can't ignore it. She's talented, connected, and she didn't deserve to be treated like that. If she's willing to stand up, she needs protection—or at least a safe way to pass information."

Pell studied him. "And you wouldn't mind being the one to give her that protection, would you?"

He gave a small, wry smile. "Maybe not. She deserves better than Charles. I don't know if that makes me her rescuer or just someone who hates seeing good people crushed. Either way, I'll be careful."

Pell smiled faintly. "Be careful. For all our sakes, nephew."

Ned nodded just as Daniel came into his room.

"Hello, Pell. I just told Mama, but please come out to the ranch for dinner tomorrow. Mama says you both have an idea for us, and you can check up on this guy."

"I would be delighted. Thank you, Daniel, for everything."

Chapter Eleven
Dinner at Daniel's Ranch

By the next evening, Pell and Mimi had spent the better part of the day digging into the Weirton Steel Mill Employee Stock Ownership Plan, or ESOP for short. They had read articles, dug up archived news reports, and watched interviews with union leaders and workers. Enough, they thought, to explain the basic idea without getting lost in technicalities. They both knew that most of the people they were about to talk to were too young to remember the original steel mill ESOP or even the concept. Mimi's eyes lit up when she found a polished YouTube video that summarized it in seven minutes flat—clear, concise, and even a little inspiring.

"This will definitely do nicely," Pell said, sipping her coffee and leaning back in her chair. "No one has to tell you people respond to stories, Mimi. Numbers are fine, but stories stick."

Mimi nodded. "It's almost too perfect. Short, to the point, and they use actual workers explaining it themselves. They'll see it's possible."

By dusk, they loaded their notes and Pell's laptop into Mimi's car and headed up the dirt road to Daniel's ranch. The way wound through a dense corridor of trees, the fading light slanting across leaves like molten gold. Fall had arrived. The ranch house itself emerged gradually: a sprawling stone and log cabin, fireplaces visible through large windows. Inside, a wide, sunken living room gave the impression of being both grand enough for business and cozy enough for family gatherings. Mimi mentioned that the powwow grounds lay some distance beyond the house, a reminder of the traditions the Tobey family valued and protected.

From the kitchen, the smell of roasting vegetables and fresh bread mixed with the soft aroma of pine from the cabin beams. Cliff was already there with his wife Dawn and their two children, Hope and Tobias, who were playing with a scattering of toys on the hearth. Toby, age six, wore a dinosaur T-shirt and a grin that suggested he knew he was soon to have a special day. Hope, four, clutched a stuffed rabbit while casting wide-eyed glances at Pell, who was carrying a tray of her own homemade cookies. Cliff and Dawn watched, amused, as their children approached Pell as if she were a celebrity.

"Ms. Pell! Is that really you?" Toby asked, bouncing on the balls of his feet.

"The lady who lives in the train?" Hope added, echoing his curiosity.

"Yes, that would be me," Pell said, smiling down at them. There was a strange delight in hearing children frame her life as a kind of legend.

"Can we go on the train?" Toby asked eagerly. "My birthday's tomorrow!"

Pell leaned in closer. "I'd love for you to visit, and Hope and your mom too, but your dad and DH make the train go. Let's see what they think." She looked over at the men. "Cliff, DH, can the yard engine tow the Pullman a short way for a birthday ride?"

DH's deadpan expression softened, just slightly, into a half-smile. "Short way? I can make it a magical mile if you want."

Toby's face lit up, Hope clapped her hands, and even DH allowed a rare laugh to escape. Pell noticed Cliff exchanging a glance with DH — a fleeting acknowledgment of shared pride and planning. A party, Pell thought. This is exactly the sort of thing this place—and the line—needed. The children were on to something. The Pullman wasn't just a vehicle; it could be a draw, a small source of fun and revenue, a way to connect with people. Someone should have some fun around here. And if Pell had any say in it, that someone was going to be her.

Daniel served dinner at an expandable table long enough to comfortably seat them all. Pell took a moment to appreciate the scene: the flicker of fire-light, the warmth of family and friends gathering, the ease with which the children laughed and played. DH sat quietly, passing a dish of roasted vegetables to Cliff, who in turn offered it to Daniel, who had taken a seat at the head of the table. There was a rhythm to the evening, a sense of casual respect underlaid with deep familiarity.

After plates were cleared and the children settled with coloring books, Mimi leaned toward Pell. "They're ready," she whispered, eyes sparkling.

"Wi-Fi?" Pell asked Daniel, half-joking.

Daniel chuckled. "I can do better than Wi-Fi." He stood, gesturing for everyone to follow, and led them into the sunken living and conference room. He hooked up Pell's laptop, flipped on the projector, dimmed the lights, and in moments the YouTube video glowed across the large screen over the fireplace.

The group watched quietly, the black-and-white, seven-minute video playing like a spark waiting to catch. Workers described how owning the company had changed their lives, how they'd been able to influence decisions, improve safety, and even raise wages. Pell noticed Daniel leaning forward slightly, fingers interlaced, while Ned's eyebrows lifted as if he were just realizing something obvious but revolutionary. Cliff's jaw tightened briefly, reflecting concentration and perhaps cautious hope. DH's expression remained careful, yet his half-smile hinted that he recognized potential in the plan.

When the video ended, Pell and Mimi rose. Pell's voice carried, confident but inviting. "This," she said, sweeping a hand toward the screen, "is what we're talking about doing. Not exactly, but close enough to understand the principle. We think… we could do something similar. Take over the North South rail and company. Make it a real, working example of employee ownership."

Mimi added, "It could work if we organize. Everyone up and down the line could invest. Control our own destiny."

Pell continued, her eyes scanning the group. "I'm willing to mortgage my home to buy stock. If we all commit what we can, and by all I mean everyone, not just us, we really could make this happen."

Daniel and Ned exchanged a look, a silent acknowledgment passing between two seasoned businessmen. This could work!

DH and Cliff murmured among themselves. Ownership, control over repairs, maybe even wages — there was a tangible excitement in their discussion, the sort that comes from realizing a solution is actually within reach. Where the union had failed, this might succeed.

Ned's voice cut through the chatter. "We could get proxies, too. Encourage stockholders to vote with us. That's how you take control legally, without confrontation."

Daniel nodded. "If we get a viable plan together and the numbers make sense, I would invest too—on behalf of the tribe."

"But what if the pulp and paper mills go out of business?" Ned asked. His concern was practical, grounded.

Pell smiled, shaking her head. "Things have changed since the days when they were the only customers. Up and down the line's 800 miles, there are more businesses now that could use rail services. And we could even add passenger service again."

Mimi leaned in. "It used to exist, you know. As a girl, I rode with my mother all the way to North Carolina and back. I heard the company canceled it because of insurance worries. But the demand never really went away."

DH, ever practical, interjected. "Freight pays better than passengers. Always has. But passenger service has value — brand value, community engagement. We could add a passenger car."

The room fell into a thoughtful silence. Hope and Toby were now quietly coloring, unaware that the adults around them were planting the seeds of a plan that could change lives. Pell felt a rare warmth, the kind that comes from aligning vision with action, from seeing possibility where before there was only inertia.

"So," Pell said finally, letting her gaze travel across the room, "It feels like we have a plan. It's not all worked out yet. But it's real, and we're out of the shadows. We can act. Together."

A murmur of agreement rippled through the group. Ned nodded, Daniel's hands tightened into a contemplative clasp, and DH allowed himself a small, approving nod. Even Cliff's usual cautious posture seemed more relaxed, as if the weight of indecision had lifted.

Outside, the light of the rising moon shone from behind the trees, and the distant sounds of the ranch — the murmur of the wind through pines, a dog barking — underscored the moment. Pell felt the pulse of it, the subtle thrill of a new beginning. Tonight, they weren't just dreaming. Tonight, they were deciding.

When Mimi and Pell were in the car headed to her house, Mimi said, "We did it. The idea caught fire. Everyone's on board, at least emotionally."

Pell nodded. "Now comes the hard work. But it feels good to finally have hope. Real hope not just wishes. We can finally take control and make something lasting, and — just maybe — have some fun along the way."

Mimi smirked. "Speaking of fun… we'd better get a cake baked and the Pullman decorated first thing in the morning."

Pell groaned in mock horror. "Who knew running a revolution also required streamers and frosting?"

Mimi laughed. "All part of the job description. Let's call it morale management."

The Pullman awaited. Tomorrow, it would roll — not just for a birthday ride, but as the first step of a movement that no one in that room would forget.

Chapter Twelve
War!

The Pullman sat gleaming in the late-afternoon sun, a little too fine for the battered pulp and paper cars coupled in front of it. Someone had polished the brass rail on the rear platform until it caught the light like a beacon, and a string of balloons bobbed from the stanchions—gifts from Dawn Tobey for the town's children. It was Toby's birthday, after all, and if DH and Cliff were going to tow the Pullman up and down the short siding, then by gosh, the boy was going to get a parade.

Inside, children pressed their faces to the salon's tall windows as the train inched forward. Cliff, wearing his conductor's cap only slightly askew, gave a mock salute to the gathered families lining the track. The engine barely covered a tenth of a mile before returning, but to Toby, it might as well have been a cross-country adventure. The little boy stood tall at the end of the ride, arms raised in triumph, flushed with excitement and the kind of triumph that can only come from being seen, celebrated, and elevated just for a moment.

Afterward, children crowded around the dining table inside the Pullman. Mimi handed out paper party hats while Dawn passed cake slices. Laughter filled the car as Toby blew out his candles, his cheeks shiny with frosting. Even Daniel had put his phone away, his tie loosened, a rare smile crossing his face as he stood beside Ned, who looked half-exhausted and half-thrilled at the success of the tiny parade.

"Not bad for a railroad supposedly running out of steam," Ned said, watching the scene through the open rear door, his voice soft but filled with pride.

Daniel followed his gaze. "Half the town came out just to see it move," he said. "That's what you're selling—not just stock. A sense of belonging. If you want this ESOP thing to breathe, you've got to make people feel like they already own a piece of it."

"Then we lead with that," Ned said. "Forget the numbers at first—start with this. Cake, balloons, a train. It's memory-making stuff. It's the heartbeat of the community, the thing no spreadsheet can ever capture."

Pell caught Ned's eye and smiled. It was good to see him alive again, not just reacting to disaster but helping shape something new. The boy who had run from responsibility, the man who had once crumpled under pressure, was now fully present, fully engaged. She let herself feel that spark of hope—quiet, fragile, and warm.

Later, when the last balloons began to sag and the Pullman's guests had drifted home, Pell joined Daniel and Ned at the ranch house. Daniel cleared a space on the dining table and unrolled a wide sheet of butcher paper. Ned paced nearby, hands jammed into his pockets, his steps punctuating the heavy silence that came with planning a small war.

"This is where we draw up the plan," Daniel said. "Off-site. No risk of corporate ears picking up the signal."

Ned leaned over the paper. "Charles and Granger are already scheming. If we wait for the spring shareholders' meeting, it'll be too late. They'll twist arms to get proxies, offer promises, drain the place dry without anyone knowing until it's done."

"Then we don't wait," Daniel said firmly. "We start pulling proxies now. If we control enough shares ahead of time, they won't be able to stop it. We've got to beat them at their own game."

Ned nodded. "We need a pitch. One that hits people where they live. Pride. Legacy. Community. Something that makes them stand up and say: 'I will not let this slip through my fingers.'"

Pell sipped her coffee and listened, a bemused smile tugging at her lips. The two men—once rivals of a kind—were now strategizing like startup founders in a dusty old train movie. It might've been funny if it weren't so damn serious.

"Also," Ned added grimly, "we need to warn share-holders about stock watering. They'll promise value, then dilute the shares behind everyone's back."

"Let's build that into the message," Daniel said. "Choose the ESOP, keep your stock safe. Stick with the current board, and you gamble everything. Tell them what's at stake, plainly."

The next day, while Pell swept cake crumbs from the Pullman's floor, her phone rang. Marissa's voice, sharp and shaken, came through like static in a storm.

"I can't get anything on paper," she whispered. "No receipts, no memos—but I heard them, Pell. Charles and Granger. They're gathering proxies. Fast. Planning to sell assets and borrow heavy to buy more stock. They also mentioned watering the stock—but I don't know what that means."

Pell felt her stomach tighten. "It means everyone's shares lose value. Yours, Ned's, Daniel's—everyone's. That's how they win without looking like thieves."

There was a pause. Then: "Pell... he's watching me. Charles. He's sticking to me like a shadow. I don't feel safe. I need out. Can I come to you?"

"Yes," Pell said instantly. "If you can lose him, come here. We'll hide you."

After she hung up, Pell called Daniel and Ned. "Marissa called. She' coming here if she can get away. And it's on," she told them. "They're playing dirty."

"A proxy war," Daniel said, his voice grim. "It's got to happen. And we need to buy up stock as fast as we can."

Ned swore under his breath. "We can't wait anymore. Every shareholder we talk to, they'll already be spinning to get signatures first."

"We counter it," Pell said. "Truth, before they poison the well."

Daniel nodded. "Then we need a story. Something they can see and feel."

"A video," Ned said suddenly. "Like the one from the steel mill. Marissa's trained. She can do it."

"She's not safe here," Pell countered. "After all, they found Ned. You, DH, and Cliff are heading south tomorrow. She'll come home with me. We'll base out of my house at the end of the line. Shoot the film. Put together the video. Quietly."

Daniel looked at her, then nodded. "It works. But everyone needs to keep their mouth shut."

"And their eyes open," Pell added.

That evening, as dusk crept across the tracks, Marissa slipped onto the Pullman with a single hard-sided suitcase and her camera gear bag. She wore black jeans, a dark hoodie, and sneakers—her face pale but resolute. DH helped her inside then pulled down the shades throughout the car.

"I told Charles my mother had a fall," she said. "And I checked everything. No bugs, no trackers." She locked eyes with Pell. "I'm not going back."

"Good! You're safe here," Pell said. "Go settle into my compartment. Then come out for dinner—we've got a lot to talk about."

"I'll hide her car," DH said, already heading outside.

The next morning, the Pullman rolled south. At the container paper plant, DH and the engineer eased the train to a halt beside the platform. Ned, DH, and Cliff stepped out, greeting the plant operations manager and rail workers. They didn't waste time. They spoke openly about what was happening—about ownership, dignity, and the chance to make the railroad something more than a dying utility.

Some workers listened, skeptical. Others nodded slowly, arms crossed but interested. A few even asked, "Where do we sign?"

Meanwhile, inside the Pullman, Marissa opened her laptop and spread paper across the dining table.

She and Pell sketched out a storyboard: interviews showing the potential benefits of ownership and the harm of letting it all go, overhead shots of mills, footage of the line stretching across the landscape and all the people it touched.

"You've got a good eye for this," Pell said, impressed with Marissa's ability to turn words into visual communications that grabbed the eye and heart.

She looked up at Pell, gratitude in her eyes. "Thank you. I've been waiting to make something real," Marissa replied. "This matters."

At Pell's house in North Carolina, Marissa worked late into the nights, Pell assisting when needed, tinkering in her miniatures workshop and resting when not. They took careful drives out to the mills—always checking their mirrors, always scanning the road behind them.

Workers came willingly to talk with them, sitting on milk crates or leaning on pallets, telling stories: how their grandfathers had laid track and built boxcars, how their uncles had driven engines. Some wiped their eyes when talking about the fear of losing it all.

"They take and take," one woman said, her voice brittle. "We build it, and they drain it like it's nothing. If this ESOP can stop that—I'll do whatever it takes."

Marissa filmed it all.

Each evening, Pell made dinner while Marissa crafted a compelling video from the footage. Ned stopped by some nights when he was near, his coat damp with rain or road dust, exhausted but buzzing.

"Got six more signatures today," he'd say one night, victorious.

The next: "We lost one. Charles sent them a letter—sweet promises. They bought it. I also heard they delivered a big load of building material to the Tobewanaki station and bull-dozed the debris down to the foundation."

DH was skeptical. "Or maybe they are implying they're going to make a few building jobs happen for goodwill. I'll believe it when I see it."

Daniel called often, muttering over spreadsheets. "If they dilute before the meeting, we'll need more capital than we thought. But if we lock down just forty-three percent, we're the biggest bloc. The rest are too split to stop us."

Pell frowned. "Forty-three doesn't sound like winning."

"It is," Daniel said, tapping his pen. "In a fractured room, a solid bloc rules the day."

In the background, DH raised an eyebrow. "Sounds to me like we need to show up in force."

Throughout the next weeks, the race was on, full steam ahead.

By the time the leaves had almost finished falling in North Carolina, Pell and Marissa had completed a rough cut of the video. In under ten minutes, it captured what they had heard again and again: the line mattered. The jobs mattered. And the chance to own it? That could mean everything.

It was time to return north. Pell and Marissa boarded the Pullman just after dawn. The plan was simple: rejoin DH, Cliff, and Ned, gather Mimi's feedback on the video back on the Tobewanaki lands, and start preparing for the final push toward the spring meeting.

Once the Pullman was in place on its siding beside the old Tobewanaki station, Mimi greeted them with brisk energy, full of preparations for the upcoming Native American Festival. She'd previewed the rough cut of the ESOP video, catching a minor audio glitch and a mislabeled mill shot. Relieved to have Mimi's approval, Marissa made the correction. "Now this will speak," Mimi said.

"And by the way, you women are staffing the ESOP tent in the vendor's area during the visitor's day. Show the video, hand out copies, answer questions. Make it part of the day, not a separate pitch."

Pell, knowing better than to get in the way of a woman on a mission, said only, "Just show us where to go."

Early on the morning of the festival, Pell and Marissa traveled with DH to the powwow grounds on the land behind Daniel's house. Vendors were already busy setting up tents for crafts, frybread stalls, and beadwork. Daniel was everywhere on his horse, securing tents, ensuring porta johns and parking happened in order and were put in the right places.

Cliff and some of his friends rode the perimeter, discreetly providing security.

As the day progressed, and people began weaving through the vendors tents and stopping by their tent, Pell and Marissa played the video on loop, laughing when curious children pressed their noses to the screen, answering questions from adults about the chance to secure ownership of the railroad. They handed out video copies and *What to Do Next* flyers and asked everyone interested to show their friends and colleagues back home.

As the day drew to a close, Pell heard Mimi's voice announcing the final dance, the friendship dance open to all. The drums began again, and the rhythm carried joy through the air. Pell felt it in her chest, a lightness she hadn't known for weeks. Remembering DH's words, Pell made her way to the circle. There was DH clapping along, his usual stoic face cracking into smiles as he stepped into the circle. Side by side, Pell and DH danced together spinning and laughing, blending into the circle of tribe members and friends, for a moment, at one with each other and their world.

As night fell, Pell and DH drifted toward the firepit in the camping area, hoping to find Ned. She spotted him seated with Marissa, wrapped together in a big plaid blanket. They were absorbed in quiet conversation, oblivious to her presence. Smiling softly, Pell gestured to DH to turn back. They headed to the Pullman, leaving Ned and Marissa to their warmth and closeness. Seeing them together carried a mix of joy, relief, and the gentle ache of impending challenges ahead. Pell was reminded again that she would not be here forever. At least Ned might have a chance for a life beyond just the railroad.

Winter was on the horizon, and the work ahead was far from done. Yet today—the powwow, the drumming and dancing, the shared labor—had etched lines of connection, delicate but unbreakable, across family, community, and tribe. Those lines would carry them, tethered to one another, into the promise of spring.

Chapter Thirteen
The Caravan

Winter had been merciless, but Pell Mell, DH, Cliff, Ned, and Marissa treated it like a personal challenge. Snowstorms, frozen switches, and the occasional grumpy stockholder did little to slow them down. They train pressed south delivering pulp and back north again with finished paper and cardboard, the Pullman rattling at the end of the freight cars, carrying the ESOP mission along.

From Maine to the Carolinas, they moved ceaselessly, visiting everyone who might own a share of the North-South Pulp and Paper Railroad. Each meeting was its own little adventure. Pell kept a running tally of excuses for not signing and exasperated, made up a few of her own to share with DH.

"'My cat chewed the paperwork,'" she said one night, warming her hands over the Pullman's stove. "'I can't vote without my bridge club approval.' And my personal favorite—'I'm on a diet and can't digest corporate politics.'"

DH smirked, not looking up from the stack of proxy forms he was sorting. "You forgot the one about the man who said he couldn't sign because Mercury was in retrograde."

"That one was real!" Marissa protested from the opposite seat, where she and Ned were cross-referencing names with addresses. "He showed me his horoscope to prove it."

"Then it must be true," Pell said dryly.

By March, the winter had hardened into a mosaic of victories and minor skirmishes: a small Maine family convinced only after Pell promised they could name a freight car after their late uncle; a factory manager in Georgia swayed by DH's combination of gruff charm and relentless practicality; and countless others, each added to the growing web of proxies. Daniel and Ned kept count, arranging all the financing they could find in the background.

The Pullman bore the chaos of the campaign: boxes of paperwork stacked in every corner, folding chairs leaning like drunks against the walls, winter coats draped over the backs of velvet couches. Sometimes the car doubled as a traveling circus: cousins, children, suspicious dogs, and one goat—"a witness to the signing," its owner insisted—had all passed through.

Cliff shook his head one night as he tried to clear a path through the mess. "From executive car to paper warehouse to livestock barn. Pell, you're really bringing out the Pullman's full résumé."

"Just wait till the summer," Pell said. "We'll add tomato farming to the list."

As the days lengthened, the campaign reached its crescendo. A caravan began to form, a slow-moving river converging on the Maine headquarters. DH and Cliff scavenged every rail yard they knew to find usable passenger cars. They patched together what they could: a string of old coaches, creaking and groaning but fit enough to serve. Volunteers painted them with hastily scrawled slogans declaring *ESOP Power!* and *Vote for North-South Community Rail!*

Each rail yard became a staging ground. Stockholders, employees, and curious neighbors crowded into the cars, rented buses, and caravanned in pickup trucks towing RVs. DH and Cliff coordinated the chaos, issuing instructions, handing out agendas and maps, signaling engineers with sharp, precise gestures. DH did it all with his usual laconic calm, but Pell noticed the way his jaw worked overtime, the way his eyes tracked every moving part.

"Lot of trouble just to sit in a meeting," DH muttered to her one morning as they watched a family wrestle luggage, a fiddle case, and a turkey into a coach.

"You mean democracy?" Pell replied. "Yes, a dreadful inconvenience. You know the old saying though. If you want to travel fast, go alone. If you want to travel far, go with others. And DH, we're going all the way!"

The caravan's arrival in the Maine railyard was nothing short of spectacular. Frost still rimed the morning grass, but the Pullman gleamed like it had been waiting all winter for this moment. Its brass rails caught the sunlight and threw it back in a golden flash.

Behind it stretched the patched-together coaches, clattering like tin toys. The banners flapped proudly, paint still wet in places. The engineer blasted the whistle as they rolled into the yard, and a cheer went up from the passengers.

Derek, the yardmaster, stood at attention as if reviewing troops, arms crossed, his thin mustache twitching with amusement. Beside him, Cliff was already barking orders.

"Unload carefully, people! Tents on the north lawn, latrine to the back. Somebody find out where the coffee went—before I lose my mind!"

Passengers spilled out, blinking in the bright light, stretching stiff legs, lugging coolers and camping stoves. Some headed for town; others began hammering stakes into the ground right in the yard. DH and Pell commandeered his truck, with Marissa squeezed in the middle, to shuttle people back and forth in the bed.

By evening, the rail yard and headquarters grounds resembled a county fair more than a corporate meeting. Early arrivals had claimed spots on the lawn, rail sidings, and any patch of ground that offered elevation. Town restaurants, agile enough to smell opportunity, dispatched food trucks to the encampments. The hardware store stayed open long past dark to sell tarps, lanterns, and anything else they could.

It was festive, but not everyone felt safe. As Pell climbed back into the Pullman to catch her breath, she found Marissa sitting rigid on the sofa, her hands clasped tightly in her lap.

"What's wrong, dear?" Pell asked, lowering herself beside her.

Marissa's eyes flicked to the window, where the glow of tents and campfires lit the night. "He's there, isn't he? Charles. He'll be in that meeting tomorrow. I've been signing papers and making calls all winter, but the thought of looking him in the eye..." She trailed off, her knuckles white.

Pell laid a hand on her arm. "You've already faced worse than Charles, and you're still here. He's just a man in a suit with too much money and too little imagination."

Marissa gave a shaky laugh. "Easy for you to say."

"Not easy," Pell corrected gently. "But true. And here's what's different from last time. You won't be alone tomorrow."

Inside the elegant railroad headquarters, Charles stood at the window of his corner office, fuming. Tents had sprouted on the manicured lawn like weeds. Smoke curled from a fire circle, where someone was leading a chorus of "This Land Is Your Land" on an accordion.

"This is trespassing," Charles snapped, turning to Granger. "Unlawful assembly. Disorderly conduct. Call the police."

The police chief—a broad-shouldered man with a permanent sunburn—was summoned. He stood in Charles's office, hat in hand, chewing gum with leisurely defiance.

"I can arrest a few," he said at last, "but I can't arrest enthusiasm."

"Do it anyway," Charles barked.

The chief nodded and ambled out. Within the hour, a half-dozen "rowdy" supporters were rounded up. But instead of cells, they found coffee, sandwiches, and an unlocked door. By nightfall, the holding area had become a makeshift hostel.

One stockholder, a woman from South Carolina, declared it "the nicest night I've ever spent in jail."

Pell, hearing of this later, remarked with wry amusement: "The chief's hospitality exceeds anything I experienced at the hotel. They should take notes."

The next morning, Granger tried to soothe Charles's temper.

"Charles, with respect," he said carefully, "if you arrest them all, you'll only make martyrs. What we need is to win votes, not create resentment."

Charles scowled, but the point was taken. Soon, workers were setting up a massive barbecue buffet on the wraparound porch of headquarters. Porta-johns and wash stations arrived with comic speed.

When the food came, Charles, Granger, and their allies rolled up their sleeves and manned the serving tables.

"Smile," Granger hissed under his breath. "Pretend they're family."

Charles handed out plates of ribs, his jaw locked in a rictus grin. "Welcome," he muttered through gritted teeth, "to the great tradition of the North-South Railroad."

From the lawn, Pell raised a cup of sweet tea in his direction, her eyes glinting with mischief.

But as the sun slipped behind the trees and lanterns were lit across the encampments, the mood shifted. Word spread that unfamiliar men had been drifting through the crowd, whispering offers of cash for proxies.

Cliff, already prowling the perimeter like a watchdog, caught sight of one near the Pullman. The man had cornered a young employee, a two-year veteran of the line, and was pressing an envelope into his hand.

"Problem?" Cliff's voice was low, almost friendly.

The operative looked up, startled. "Private business."

Cliff stepped closer, his shoulders filling the space like a wall. "Not here it isn't."

When the man tried to shove past him, Cliff moved fast, grabbing his arm and twisting him into the side of a boxcar with a thud that echoed through the yard. The employee bolted.

"Tell Charles," Cliff growled into the man's ear, "that if he wants to fight, he can show up tomorrow like the rest of us. He sends any more rats into the camps tonight, I won't just pin their arms."

By the time Cliff released him, the operative had gone pale. He stumbled off into the dark. The others who had been working the camp melted away within minutes.

When Cliff returned to the Pullman, dusting off his hands, Pell arched an eyebrow. "Security detail?"

"Somebody's got to keep the circus safe," he said simply.

That night, the camp buzzed like a fairground. Lanterns and campfires flickered in the spring air, fiddles and guitars competed with laughter, and food trucks hummed like carnival rides. The Pullman sat gleaming at the edge of it all, windows glowing softly.

Inside, Pell and DH had collapsed into the parlor chairs, boots off, coats slung over the back of the sofa. Ned and Marissa were at the dining table bent over yet another stack of proxy forms, whispering and laughing. Cliff leaned against the wall, arms crossed, scanning the windows now and again as though he expected another visitor.

Pell poured two fingers of whiskey into a coffee mug and lifted it to the group. "To democracy," she said.

Without looking up, DH responded, "To survival."

For a moment the noise outside faded, leaving only the faint clatter of the heater and the soft breathing of the car.

"You think we've done enough?" Pell asked at last, her voice lower, edged with fatigue.

DH rubbed his jaw, then nodded. "We've done all anybody could. Tomorrow—it's theirs."

Pell smiled faintly. "That's the point, isn't it?"

Ned looked up from the table, grinning. "It sure is, but don't go sentimental on us, Aunt Pell. We've got a revolution in the morning."

"Revolutions require sleep," Marissa added firmly, stacking the forms with a snap. "Bedtime for all generals, effective immediately."

Pell leaned back, her eyes heavy but her pulse quick with anticipation. Outside, voices still rose in song and laughter, the camp alive with expectation.

Tomorrow the fight would be decided. Tonight, they let themselves rest in the warmth of their unlikely fellowship.

Chapter Fourteen
Stockholder's Meeting

The next day dawned brisk and clear, the kind of spring morning that made the scent of the nearby ocean sharp and alive. Sunlight streaked through the tall windows of the elegant stone headquarters, glinting off polished wood and crystal chandeliers in a building that had once been a monument to corporate opulence. The room itself seemed to shimmer with history, every carved molding and pane of glass a witness to decades of deals, arguments, and ambition. In what was now the meeting hall, folding chairs lined the walls; people perched precariously on windowsills, and a few daring souls had climbed onto the back tables, straining to glimpse the center of the room where the board sat, surrounding a conference phone. The faint smell of polished wood mingled with paper and coffee, creating a heady atmosphere of anticipation.

Daniel's communications van from Singing Wire sat outside, a tangle of cables snaking into the hall like metallic vines. With Marissa at his side, he had rigged a makeshift broadcast system, streaming audio and visuals to every corner of the grounds. Those who couldn't squeeze inside the hall—on lawns, in cafes, even behind drawn curtains in homes nearby—watched and listened on computers, tablets, and phones, leaning forward as if their physical proximity might somehow tip the balance. The air was taut with expectation, a quiet hum of static electricity between hope and fear.

The meeting began with the kind of careful formality expected in a corporate setting. Charles Haskell, resplendent in a navy suit and a tie that might have been a little too tight, adjusted his cufflinks with deliberate precision and addressed the crowd. "Ladies and gentlemen," he said, his voice booming and tinged with authority, "we are gathered here according to the agenda previously distributed. Let us proceed with decorum and civility. We have a vote scheduled—"

A ripple of murmurs ran through the room, a chorus of skepticism and restrained impatience. Charles's face tightened. "—and I will remind everyone that any attempt to disrupt this process, or to ignore the procedural rules, will not be tolerated. If necessary, I will clear this hall in the name of order."

That was the moment Ned appeared. He strode into the hall with Marissa by his side, her camera slung over one shoulder, a calm confidence in her step that seemed to ripple through the crowd. Charles's eyes flicked up, and for the first time that morning, the red tinge in his face deepened, almost physically emanating heat.

"Ah," Charles said, forcing a smile that didn't reach his eyes. "Mr. Talmadge. And Ms. Sadler—your associate?"

"Yes, she's with me," Ned replied, voice steady, carrying an edge that unsettled Haskell and, subtly, the onlookers. A few stockholders leaned forward, sensing the tension and tasting the faint thrill of a fight brewing between the two men.

The hall seemed to tighten around them, a collective inhale as if the room itself waited for the inevitable spark. Ned and Charles squared off, a kind of measured fury building in the space between them. Charles jabbed a finger at Ned, his voice rising. "This vote is invalid! You have no right—"

"I have every right," Ned cut in, his words precise, resonant. "And I'm not going to let you intimidate these stockholders. The proxies are legitimate. We're moving forward."

Chaos rippled quickly through the room. Accusations ricocheted, legal jargon clashing with raw indignation. Charles's red face matched the heat in his words, each sentence more pompous and insistent than the last. Ned, fueled by righteous anger—and perhaps a touch of inherited bravado—met every point with calm defiance. The tension had teeth that snapped at the edges of every participant. A folding chair wobbled dangerously near a stockholder's foot, papers rustled like dry leaves in a storm, and the murmur of voices climbed into a low roar.

From inside the Pullman, Pell Mell watched via the broadcast, hands wrapped around a steaming cup of coffee. She leaned back against the velvet couch, amused. The tension was exquisite, teetering on the line between family quarrel and corporate warfare, and she let herself savor it, heart thrumming with the private awareness of what was at stake beyond the room.

Daniel stepped forward at the front, holding a stack of documents. "We present the proxies collected, totaling thirty-nine percent of the shares," he announced clearly. The room murmured, some eyes widening, some darting to their phones. Charles's lips tightened. "Thirty-nine percent," he repeated, incredulous. "Insufficient. The vote cannot proceed—"

But Ned raised a hand, quiet yet commanding. "It will proceed. These stockholders will be heard. That's the vote. We're moving forward."

The first round of votes unfolded. Thirty-nine percent—it wasn't enough. A cloud of doubt flickered across the faces of minor stockholders and online viewers alike. Pell sipped her coffee, savoring the tension, noting the subtle shifts in posture, the twitch of a hand, the tightening jaw. Every detail mattered. Yet even in that moment of apparent setback, a faint current of anticipation hummed through her.

Then, slowly, one by one, stockholders called in— over Zoom, by phone, live feeds pinging in from distant towns. Each contribution nudged the total upward: forty percent... forty-one... forty-two...

forty-three… and finally forty-four percent. The hall exhaled collectively, a sound half disbelief, half elation. Small cheers broke out, pockets of applause mingling with relieved laughter.

Daniel's face broke into a grin. "We've done it," he said quietly, as Marissa adjusted microphones to capture every moment live. Cameras clicked, phones recorded, and the swell of triumph became almost tangible.

Ned stepped forward, calm but electric with anticipation. "All right," he said, voice carrying across the room, "the vote will be taken again." Stockholders immediately responded, ballots filled, intentions marked, a chorus of civic action swelling into an overwhelming tide.

The old board had expected compliance, resignation, quiet acceptance—but the vote was overwhelming. Cheers erupted, papers fluttered into the air like confetti. Laughter, cries, and applause mingled with Marissa's crackling broadcast, her voice dancing between disbelief and exhilaration. Charles Haskell's face drained of color. "This… this isn't valid! I demand—"

"Sit down, Charles," Ned interrupted, hand raised, calm but absolute. "You'll want to hear this. The paperwork you sent from Granger? The fraudulent stuff he tried to slip past us? Already handled. Sent to everyone, transparently. Your tricks won't stick." Granger, seated beside Haskel, went pale and rose from his seat. Without a word, he stepped toward the nearest exit and was gone.

A brief, electrified silence fell. Then a chuckle, low and triumphant, passed between Daniel and Ned. Then, the crowd burst into cheers and began flooding onto the broad porch wrapping the building. Cliff and DH moved like conductors in a storm, shepherding stockholders, preventing crushes, and redirecting the tide of human energy with quiet authority.

Pell brought her computer outside, and from her perch on the Pullman platform, listened as the camp burst into cheers. Pell joined in, heart hammering in rhythm with the tumult below. On screen, the entire town watched as Security personnel surged through the hall, papers fluttered like startled birds. And then Ned, moving with calculated momentum, shoved Charles backward. The board chair toppled into a precarious stack of folding chairs, the room ringing with a collision that was part slapstick, part symbolic triumph. Pell's laughter was unrestrained.

By nightfall, the chaotic ending of the ESOP meeting had made its way onto local news. Footage of Charles Haskell flying—quite literally—into a stack of folding chairs dominated the broadcast. Anchors struggled to maintain composure as clips replayed, stockholders cheering, papers tumbling, and Marissa's live feed crackling with excitement.

Despite the formalities still pending, the spirit of rebellion was undeniable. The Pullman, polished and gleaming, became a beacon at the center of the rail yard, a moving locus of celebration. Candles flickered in the windows, casting warm light across faces flushed with triumph. Instruments emerged from boxes, tentative at first, then joined by laughter and song. Stockholders, employees, and allies toasted to their audacity, sharing stories of winter's labor, small victories, and moments of quiet defiance.

From her vantage point on the Pullman's platform, Pell watched DH and Cliff move fluidly among the crowd—calming minor disputes, sharing small jokes. Pride stirred quietly in her chest, not just for the vote's success, but for the collective effort it represented, the living proof of what people could achieve when they worked together.

Ned climbed aboard and leaned against the polished rail with her, letting out a long breath. "You know Aunt Pell," he said, shaking his head with a grin, "Ben Franklin, right after signing the Constitution, stepped outside to a waiting crowd who asked him, "What have you wrought?" He said, "A republic, if you can keep it.""

Ned continued, "I'd like to think he'd raise a glass to us. Collective ownership, proxy votes, a train-line ESOP… not exactly what he had in mind but definitely in the right spirit."

Pell smiled at him, fingers trailing along the rail. "A fragile experiment then, and a fragile victory now. Just like a republic." Her voice held a note of wry amusement, but beneath it lay the weight of private truths—her illness, the stakes of her stewardship, the exhaustion that none around her fully saw.

Ned glanced at her, eyes narrowing. "Yeah. Fragile, and complicated. Keeping this line together… it won't be simple."

Pell's lips curved faintly. "Nothing worth doing ever is. And just look around." Pell pointed to the camp below. "Seems to me you have lots of help."

Around them, the celebration carried on, but here at the rail, a quiet understanding persisted: the work was done, but the stewardship had only just begun.

Later, in the quiet of her Pullman berth, Pell sank into the comfort of deep rest. Her heart, still buzzing faintly from the day's tumult, softened into satisfaction. She had poured herself fully into the ESOP, every choice deliberate, every effort spent. Now she could see it standing firm, a vision she had given a living form. Tomorrow, the train would roll back south, the caravan would disperse, but the line—the community—would endure. That was everything she had sought. Her work was completed.

Chapter Fifteen
To the End of the Line

The Maine railyard was still this morning. A year had passed since the ESOP takeover. Once again, Fall brushed the trees with ochre and rust. The air was sharp but clear, carrying the faint, steady wash of the tide from the coast beyond the tracks. Somewhere in the distance, a single bird called, the note lingering in the quiet. So simple, so ordinary, it seemed almost miraculous after all the noise and chaos of the year before.

The Pullman sat alone on its siding, polished and gleaming—a sentinel in the calm of early morning. Its brass trim caught the sunlight and held it, throwing sparks of gold across the gravel and ties. In the stillness, it looked less like a train car than a ceremonial carriage, waiting patiently for a procession.

Ned and DH stood a short distance away, hands in pockets, eyes tracing the newly painted letters along the car's side. *The Pell Mell*, it read, bold and bright.

"She would have hated the fuss," Ned said softly, almost to himself.

DH didn't answer immediately. He just nodded, corners of his mouth tight. "She'd have hated it but really liked the gold paint." His voice carried that low, measured weight it took to hold grief without breaking.

Ned glanced again at the letters, sunlight tracing over them. "It's ridiculous," he said, "how much life fits in one year."

DH replied, "Miraculous, maybe too."

A black van rolled in, tires crunching over gravel, easing backward with precision. Its presence cut the quiet. The doors swung open, and two men, tall and serious, drew out a modest coffin. Their black suits absorbed the light, a flat counterpoint to the Pullman's shine. DH stepped forward, gripping the corners alongside them, guiding the coffin up and inside the railcar. There was no ceremony beyond the care of the movement, a silent choreography.

Ned stayed back, hands tightening in his pockets, watching DH with renewed gratitude—for his friendship, his care for Pell Mell, his constant presence over months of shared labor, victories, and now pain. Nothing here was performative. Only the finality of what must be done.

As the van pulled away, the train from the south rumbled into the yard. The engineer leaned out from the cab, hands adjusting levers, slowing to a stop. DH, now Chief Engineer of the line, moved with mechanical precision to hook up the Pullman, checking brake lines, coupling, making sure the pulp cars were ready for the journey from north to south once more.

His face was closed, holding storm clouds behind calm eyes. "Brake lines," he said to the engineer. "Check again. Make sure the connections are tight. No surprises. We will pick up the passenger car at Tobewanaki station."

The engineer nodded, used to DH's exacting ways, and bent over his work. DH ran a hand over the Pullman's rear platform rail, lingering just a second longer than necessary, caught in a memory.

Ned watched a moment, then turned toward the headquarters building where he now worked, developing new business for the community-owned line. The old stone mansion looked unchanged, though he knew what had shifted inside. He stepped onto the porch, where the newly elected ESOP leaders and owners lingered. Though the office was technically closed, people had gathered—clusters of familiar faces murmuring softly, offering condolences, cards. Inside, the marble entry hall was filled with flowers, the air scented with lilies and chrysanthemums.

"I just wanted to say how grateful I was to know her," someone said. "She… she made it all possible."

Ned nodded, voice low. "Aunt Pell wouldn't have done it for thanks. Only to keep things running."

Back on the track, DH remained with the Pullman and the coffin, leaning against the wall, hands on the wood paneling, letting himself feel the empty ache. Inside, the Pullman was warm with residual sunlight. Bottles of whiskey and wine—Pell's favorites, always ready for guests—stood like silent temptations on the dining room sideboard. He knew the ritual, the way she had poured herself a glass when the work was done. He wanted to empty them. He remembered his deal with Pell Mell long ago. It would be like spitting in her face, but he wanted it.

DH picked up both bottles with deliberate care and stepped outside. With a heave, the bottles flew into the scrub. The sound of glass shattering felt just right and DH dusted off his hands.

Footsteps on gravel announced Ned's return. He stepped onto the platform quietly, setting his pack down. "Mind if I stay?" he asked, voice low, careful.

DH shook his head, wordless. No more was needed between old friends. Inside, Ned joined DH, both sitting opposite the coffin, silence settling around them like a blanket. They spoke nothing, sharing only the space, the memory, the weight of loss. Outside, the wind whispered through the trees, and the distant tide murmured, carrying the final echoes of a year that had changed everything.

Together, they would stay with her through the night, waiting for the morning when the train would leave, when the Pullman would begin its journey down the line, towing the cars filled with the fruits of the ESOP's labor, with the hope she had planted. In the quiet, the world seemed both impossibly large and intimately contained, every sound and shadow a tribute to the life that had passed and the work that would continue.

With a blast of the whistle, the train rolled forward with a low, steady rumble, vibrating through the ties—a pulse in the quiet afternoon. DH sat in the engineer's seat, eyes fixed on the tracks ahead, hands resting lightly on the controls. Ned rode beside him for the first time in many years, shoulders hunched, watching the autumn trees blur past. Neither spoke much. Words felt insufficient. The year's labor, the victories and losses, the laughter and sorrow—they traveled in the silence between them.

At each pulp delivery stop, small clusters of ESOP employees waited, hands folded, and eyes soft. They emerged quietly from the yards and buildings, nodding to DH and Ned, some brushing dust from their sleeves as they stepped forward. A few offered flowers or a nod of appreciation—quiet, restrained gestures, fitting the somber rhythm of the day.

"Thank you," Ned said once, voice low, almost swallowed by the whistle of wind past the railcars.

"Not for us," DH murmured back. "For her."

No one pressed further. Eyes lingered, then turned back to the train as it continued its slow, deliberate crawl south. It was a procession of remembrance, measured and patient, each stop a quiet offering.

By the time the train approached Tobewanaki Station, the sun had dipped lower, painting the sky in dusty gold and soft violet. Children ran along the grassy embankment ahead of the engine, tossing handfuls of wildflowers onto the rails. The petals tumbled across the ties, carried by a slight wind—a delicate carpet of color for the train to pass over. DH slowed the engine just enough to let the moment linger, eyes narrowing on the small figures waving with chubby, eager hands.

"Look at them," Ned said softly, almost smiling. "They know who she was."

"They know," DH said, voice low. "To them, she was the lady that lived in the train."

The station came into view, its frame tall and raw, the new wood still unpainted. Above the wide, open doors, a freshly hung sign announced: *Tobewanaki Station and North-South Community Railroad Museum.* The letters were crisp, proud, like the people who had built the place. Marissa and Mimi waited inside, hands moving over wires and fixtures with the lighting installers, setting up the gallery that would tell the real story of the tribe and the railroad.

Mimi wore a small, neatly printed nameplate: *Mimi Tobey, Cultural Liaison.* Her expression was serious, but her eyes flickered with pride as she adjusted the positioning of an overhead spotlight.

Marissa crouched near a wall, camera in hand, pausing occasionally to guide a technician, to catch the best angle of the installation. When she saw Ned approaching, she straightened, face softening, and held out her hands.

"Ned," she said, and for a moment, the work and quiet around them seemed to fall away. They met in the middle of the gallery space, a hug warm but careful, as if both were still learning to hold happiness alongside grief.

"It looks incredible," Ned said, voice quiet but steady. He stepped back, taking in the unfinished panels and raw wood, the mix of polished exhibit cases and rough-hewn benches.

"They'll get it," he continued. "Every kid who comes in here will understand why she fought so hard. Why we all did."

"I think she would be proud," Marissa said, eyes glinting. "And I think she'd like that we're telling it right. The real story." Mimi nodded.

Ned picked up the paper-wrapped picture he had brought and moved further into the station. In the next room, an HO-scale model of the North-South Community Railroad sprawled across a large table, tracks snaking along the countryside, tiny bridges arching over miniature rivers. Ripping off the paper, Ned hung Pell's portrait above the model, a reminder and a charge: volunteers welcome to help finish it. Pell smiled down on the little world as if approving.

"I'll keep it going," he whispered. "All of it."

The station smelled of fresh-cut wood, faint pine, varnish, and the warm tang of electric cables under new fixtures. Outside, the wind rustled through the leaves. The Pullman waited, patient and quiet, while DH moved to hook the passenger car onto the line, checking couplings with the meticulous care he had always shown.

"Couplings tight?" Ned called across the platform.

"Always," DH replied, voice low, a half-smile tugging at the corner of his mouth that he didn't quite let surface.

Marissa and Mimi rolled their suitcases across the wooden platform, wheels clicking softly against the boards. Standing beside Ned, Mimi said, "After all these years, riding the passenger car to North Carolina again. I wish it were for any other reason. But at least we are together."

Marissa shook her head gently, a small smile passing over her lips. "It's the right thing. We have to be with Ned—and with her. All the way." She lifted her camera case and slung it over her shoulder. "And it's the last ride she ever takes. She'd want us there."

Ned's face was calm, composed, though a tightness lingered around his eyes. The year's weight was etched into the corners of his mouth, the subtle stoop of his shoulders, the quiet way he surveyed everything.

More figures appeared. Cliff, tall and solid, stepped from the shadows near the station's far end. Now safety and security manager, he carried a protective presence in jeans and an official jacket.

Daniel followed—solid, quiet, observant—eyes scanning the horizon with the careful watchfulness of someone used to shouldering responsibility. They had come to honor Pell, and to ensure her journey continued without interruption.

As the group moved to board the passenger car, a dusty blue pickup rumbled up the gravel road to the station. The engine coughed once, then fell silent as the truck settled beside the platform. Mr. Tobey stepped down, shepherd at his side, leash unnecessary. He moved slowly, deliberately, the gait of a man whose every step was measured, respectful, and unhurried.

He reached the platform's edge and paused. His eyes, steady and grave, met Ned's. "I come with Victor's words for you. You take care of her, my good son," he said softly, voice low but carrying weight that demanded attention. Then, without another word, he nodded at Mimi and his own sons standing just behind him. Each nodded back, acknowledgment passing in a series of quiet gestures—a chain of respect and understanding. Mr. Tobey stepped away, his presence a reminder of dignity held through a lifetime of service and guardianship.

After the suitcases and personal items were stowed in the passenger car, Ned called forward. DH, already seated in the engineer's seat, responded with a blast of the whistle. Marissa adjusted her camera strap one last time, checking batteries and memory cards, though she would take few pictures. This journey was not for documentation—it was for memory, for witness, and for the act of accompaniment itself.

The train began to move, slowly at first. The wheels hummed a low, continuous note that grew in rhythm and strength. The Pullman followed, gleaming gold in the waning sunlight. The rhythm of metal on metal, steady and comforting, filled the ears of those aboard—a reminder of journeys taken and journeys yet to come.

Marissa leaned against the window, watching the station shrink, the raw wood fading into the background, tracks stretching straight and true toward the horizon. Mimi, beside her, reached out to touch the arm of the seat, fingers lingering on the smooth finish. Neither spoke. Words would have seemed foolish, intrusive, against the quiet dignity of the moment.

Outside, the train stretched like a black ribbon unwinding across the landscape, the Pullman at its end receding slowly into the distance. Tied to its platform rail, a black banner rippled in the wind, carrying the weight of memory, of the ESOP's work, of friends, family, and colleagues bound together in both labor and love. Across its dark surface, her name shone in gold lettering: *Penelope Mellors "Pell Mell" 1938–2024*, a presence both gentle and commanding, marking the legacy she laid into every mile of track behind her.

About the Author

Carol Bird tells stories about people who refuse to be limited by the systems around them, finding courage, creativity, and connection in unexpected places. Her novels celebrate the ingenuity, humor, and resilience that emerge when individuals work together to challenge constraints, solve problems, and shape their own destinies.

Pell Mell is Carol's fourth novel, following sci-fi adventure *The Time Safari Travel Company*, murder mystery *A Modest Inheritance*, and the Appalachian magical realism of *A Home Worth Having*—all available on Amazon.

When she's not writing, Carol finds inspiration wandering the waters and woods of the Chesapeake Bay region, contemplating the enigmas and possibilities that lie just beyond the surface of everyday life.

www.ingramcontent.com/pod-product-compliance
Lightning Source LLC
Chambersburg PA
CBHW020721130726
47899CB00011B/831